D0528693

When vandals struck at Shallow Dene Farm, killing and injuring many of the animals, the whole family felt the tragedy. Young Shanie was heartbroken at the loss of her pets; her aunt Frankie, who had cared for Shanie since the death of her mother, knew how much the animals had meant to her and grieved with her; Cuckoo, the stockman, was outraged at such a senseless act of cruelty. But for Sam Maddocks, Shanie's father, there was an even greater worry: a valuable brood mare had disappeared in the raid, and unless he could get the horse back, Sam and Shallow Dene Farm faced financial disaster . . .

Also by Joyce Stranger

and published by Corgi Books

Lynne Steven ce!

Joyce Stranger

Lynne Steven ce

Never Tell a Secret

Lynne Steven
Ardor Skitten
by Wick. → CAITHNESS
Scotland
Kw i wro.

CORGI BOOKS

NEVER TELL A SECRET
A CORGI BOOK 0 552 10397 7

Originally published in Great Britain by
Collins and Harvill Press

PRINTING HISTORY
Collins and Harvill edition published 1975
Corgi edition published 1977
Corgi edition reprinted 1977
Corgi edition reprinted 1980
Corgi edition re-issued 1983

This book is set in Intertype Baskerville

Corgi Books are published by
Transworld Publishers Ltd.,
Century House, 61–63 Uxbridge Road,
Ealing, London W5 5SA

Printed and bound in Great Britain by
Cox & Wyman Ltd, Reading

Especially for Nora Blackborow

CHAPTER ONE

SANDY stabbed the fire into a blaze, and looked round the room.

It was a comfortable room, spacious and well proportioned. The flaring wood flickered on large armchairs, their covers worn by the claws of generations of Siamese cats. Her latest beauties lay on the blue hearthrug, long lean legs extended, bodies turned to face the blaze. A deep contented purring filled the air.

The room should have reassured her, but somehow, it added to her fear.

She glanced out of the window. Shanie Maddock was crouched at the garden gate, facing the little wood. On another day, the child would have been in the wood, enjoying freedom.

Now, they needed to watch.

Only last week, Sandy had felt safe; here in the cottage in the quiet little lane, with so few neighbours. All her neighbours were her friends.

But someone had not been a friend.

You can't escape. You aren't safe anywhere, she told the cats. The cats purred their answer and Brunie rolled absurdly and curved a slim paw to pat at Sandy's knitting needle. The bright purple wool rolled on to the hearthrug and Liletta, forgetting her mature years, patted it thoughtfully, and watched with blue eyes that slanted wickedly as it unwound.

Sandy picked it up and put the knitting away behind the cushion. She couldn't settle. She wished it were tea time but the clock told her that there was an hour to go before it would even be decent to eat.

She picked up the newspaper again. It was three days old, but still as vivid as yesterday. The words jumped off the page, giving her the same sense of shock and outrage.

'Mr. Samuel Maddock, farmer (45) of Shallow Dene Farm, Crossley Pike, returned from a Saturday afternoon expedition to buy a new brood mare to find that vandals had visited his farm. Miss Francesca Maddock (41) stated that silver cups and jewellery were missing. Two dogs, an Alsation bitch, expecting pups, and a sheepdog, had been killed.

Cattle were injured so badly that they had to be destroyed. An in-foal mare is also missing.

'Miss Alexandra Hilton (53), a breeder of Siamese cats living at a nearby cottage, reported that she had seen four men on motor bicycles ride down the lane at two o'clock. She had been out herself for the rest of the afternoon and had heard nothing.

'Mr. Richard Turpin (58), farmhand, stated that he was at market with his employer. He knew of no one who bore the farmer a grudge, but thought that the mare might have been the reason for the attack as she is a recent acquisition, worth £5,000.

'The police are continuing their inquiries.'

Just a few paragraphs in a paper, Sandy thought. It happens every day. Robbery. And violence. But the paper doesn't tell you what happens afterwards, except to the villains. That's all reported, *if* they get caught. The victims are forgotten. There is no justice. Only law.

She looked out of the window again at Shanie, who was sitting with her fists clenched and an expression on her face that should never be seen on a twelve-year-old. Susie, the Alsatian, had belonged to the child. And the vandals had killed all the kittens in the place; Star's new babies and the tiny black kits that Shanie was hand-rearing so proudly.

The child had come to Sandy daily for advice; the mother cat had died during the birth and Sandy provided bottles and the special milk she always kept in stock lest her own queens had too little. It had been an achievement to get the kittens so far; over a month old, lively imps that already climbed to a shoulder when lifted from their box and that accepted the humans around them as foster mothers, rubbing their small heads against the chins of those that had handled them, while they tried their first tiny clicking purr that sounded more like a rattle in the throat than a cat noise.

Brunie jumped to Sandy's knee and sat staring at her with an unfathomable cat look, as if by intense probing she could discover how humans worked. Searching obviously gave her no clue, so she settled herself, after a turn around, tucking her paws neatly beneath her, giving Sandy's hand a swift loving lick before closing her eyes and starting again on her deep companionable purr. She was heavily in kit.

Sandy picked up the paper again.

It made everything remote; as if it happened to strangers,

not here, less than a quarter of a mile away, on a quiet March afternoon. Samuel Maddock, 45. Was Sam really as old as that? He must have been 33 when Sara died leaving him with a six-week-old baby daughter. Shannon. His young bride had come from Ireland and had longed to go back. She had been too fragile for a farmer's wife. Heaven knew why Sam had married her; but love did strange things. Samuel Maddock didn't sound in the least like Sam somehow! Big, bluff, and a passionate stockman who had passed on his dedication to animals to his small daughter.

And she had never realized that Frankie was really Francesca or that she was as old as 41. Did it matter? Did it have anything to do with what had happened? It had been a long time since anyone had used her own first name. Alexandra was for someone tall and stately, not a plump dumpling of a woman with a red face and sandy hair. She had to work out her own age. She didn't feel 53. She often felt eighteen and as uncertain and shy as she had been when she left school and found the city a terrifying place to live in, and decided to retreat to a country lane and breed cats.

That had worked out. Now she travelled all over the world on judging engagements, yet still found herself unnerved by trips to meet total strangers. But there were always cats at the end of the journey to restore her confidence and leap on her lap, and when she held one to assess its appearance, she forgot everything else in her total absorption, as she admired colour and points, the set of an ear, the delicacy of a leg and a paw, the bright inquisitive eyes and the full-blooded Siamese wail that she loved so much.

She knew the newspaper cutting by heart.

Fancy Cuckoo being called Richard. It didn't suit him. He had been Cuckoo for as long as she knew him, always indulging in wild schemes to make someone's fortune, always ready to sit with a calving cow, or to help when there were baby animals to be fed, or to bottle-feed a pig or a lamb. He was a widower now. His wife had been one of Sandy's greatest friends. Cuckoo lived in the tied house that went with the farm, only a stone's throw from Sandy's home. He spent much of his time training Shanie; teaching her all she would need to know when she too became a farmer. Sam had no sons.

Sandy looked out of the window again.

9

Shanie beckoned, her eyes alight with excitement for the first time for three days. She should have been at school, but she had been suffering from shock; and Sandy, who had looked after the girl while the farm was cleared up, and all evidence of the senseless attack was removed, had decided it would be better if the child had another day off. There would be too many questions; too much curiosity, and the events were too recent, and would hurt. It would go on hurting, but one learnt to adjust, though she herself was fearful now, watching the lane, hiding the cats, afraid of a personal attack.

Violence had spilled over and had marked all of them, and nothing would ever be quite the same again.

She shivered and poked the fire, and fetched her coat, to find out what Shanie wanted. The child, leaning on the gate, put a finger to her lips. Sandy trod on the grass, walking very softly, wondering what was there.

The weasel was in the middle of the narrow lane, twisting, twirling, spinning, trying to catch his tail. He somersaulted, righted himself and spun again, a whirling blur of brown-red fur, of whispering pads, and glittering watchful eyes. The little mob of fascinated birds moved close, anxious to find out what the animal was doing. They were unable to look away.

Shanie held out her hand to Sandy, knowing the cat breeder would stand for ages equally absorbed in the small importances of wild creatures. Shanie was a slender child, just twelve years old. In spite of long hours spent out of doors her face was pale, coloured only by a faint golden tan. Her deepset grey eyes were darkened by long black lashes.

She was a solemn child, often quiet, always roused to passion by any cruelty to animals. She had been brought up by her father's sister, Frankie, who had given up her own life, breeding horses in partnership, and come home to look after her brother and his child and to help with the farm where she herself had been born.

Shanie loved all animals. She shared her aunt's absorption in horses. The stolen mare was a recent acquisition, much longed for, an ambition brought to life, owned in partnership with Frankie's former fellow breeder. She had yet to tell him that the mare was gone.

Frankie and Shanie had spent hours outside the stable

every day stroking the wise head, discussing the future of the foal, speculating on its sex, planning its life. The mare leaned against them as soon as they went inside, huffing companionably, her brown eyes watching them. She always greeted them with a shrill delighted whinny and rubbed her head against them, sharing her favours between them.

For all Shanie's quietness, she was as hot-tempered as her father, and her aunt, but she and Frankie had the same sense of humour so that their rare and furious quarrels ended swiftly in laughter as both were able to see the absurdity in their own behaviour.

Sam Maddock was less easy to live with nowadays. He had farmed for all of his life; even when a boy he had busied himself with animals, hating idleness and finding small pleasure in the usual pursuits of boys. He much preferred to busy himself with the stock and now had an unerring eye for the behaviour of all his cattle and for the smaller animals too, knowing well if one ailed, or was suffering some small injury that caused a change in temper.

He was worried almost to breaking point by the world around him; by the unrealistic prices of farm animals and the astronomical cost of feed; by the endless forms and the equally endless taxes; by the difficulties imposed quite unwittingly by earnest officials obsessed with rules and regulations, governed by ideals that had nothing whatever to do with the problems of a man coping with livestock; unable to understand that though a farm might be rich in nominal value, in acres and in cattle, all of this was fool's gold, unrealizable. The land could fluctuate wildly in value, and death duties be assessed at the top of a market that fell before a sale was possible; milk prices did not reflect the cost of feed and veterinary fees; often calves were sold for a derisory sum.

Sam, when he received the feed bills, always exploded, and Shanie was terrified that her father would have a stroke, like old Mr. Malcolm opposite her school who had fallen to the pavement right under her eyes only a few months before, and had been taken to hospital, where he died.

If only life were smooth all the time.

Frankie kept the milk books, and her niece helped her. Between them they kept notes on the cows; when they were due for the bull, or the A.I. man; the expected date of the calf; the birth of the calf and any problems the cow had calving, for if you knew what to expect you could avoid big vet bills.

There were always problems.

But there had never been any like those they had now.

Shanie shuddered, and reached out to grip Sandy's hand, holding it so tightly that it hurt. Sandy said nothing. Her lips tightened and a wave of anger shook her with such force that she was almost frightened of her own rage.

Shanie watched the weasel, as if the sight could protect her from the reality that awaited her when she went home. She loved being alone, watching birds and animals; seeing the squirrels that fled through the trees, and the birds that chased them off their eggs; she knew a great deal about the hidden life of wild creatures.

She had little in common with other children, preferring the outdoor world to dancing, or watching television. Some of the girls at school seemed already grown up, yet they knew nothing at all about the real world.

They stared in astonishment if she mentioned Marylou, who lost the calfbed at every birth. Frankie had learned to insert the vital stitches that held it in place. Or if she mentioned Dulcie whose calves were invariably the wrong way round so that Spencer Dayson, the vet, had to come with the calf ropes. Marylou had been due to calve in two weeks' time. The calf had been born dead, as Marylou had been chased and worried by dogs on that dreadful Saturday afternoon. The cow was recovering slowly from her injuries.

It was better not to remember. But it was very hard to forget.

The weasel flickered in the thin sunlight that angled between the trees. There was a blackbird singing in the distance. The hawthorn buds were tightfisted in the tangled hedge, green hidden under brown except at the tips of slender buds. Bluebells thrust fleshy spear points through ground still carpeted with last year's dry dead leaves. Windflowers bowed on slim stems, yellow-eyed, their fragile petals paper-thin. There were early primroses and a few dog violets on the sheltered bank opposite the garden gate.

There was a flurry in the distant trees. Shanie counted seven magpies, holding a parliament. The noise increased, but did not distract the weasel. Seven for a secret, never to be told. She glanced at Sandy and knew the cat breeder had seen them too, and also remembered the rhyme.

The rising ground beyond was sparsely clothed with stunted saplings, sown by hoarding squirrels from the acorns that grew further down the lane on the oak tree in the Manor park that backed on to the coppice.

The birds were in a huddled circle. The weasel paused, one paw lifted from the ground, and raised his head. Thrush and blackbird and sparrow and robin watched him avidly. He moved one paw, slowly, carefully, and tensed his whippy body for the final pounce and kill.

Shanie yelled, a high yodelling cry that sent every bird skywards, wings beating in panic, and made Sandy jump. The frustrated weasel ran furiously to and fro on the ground, chittering angrily, his lithe tail lashing. He turned and saw the watchers and was gone, a memory only as he slid through the hedge and vanished.

Shanie looked at Sandy and they grinned at his miniature fury. He wouldn't go hungry long. Meanwhile the birds were safe. Shanie hated killing. She trained the farm cats to bring her their catches, and praised them extravagantly, taking the prey from them, and rewarding them with food. Rats and mice went to Cuckoo for swift dispatch and the birds went free.

There was a strange creaking above them, a grating note that sounded like a bird with a sore larynx. Shanie glanced up and nudged Sandy. There was a squirrel clinging to the trunk of the tree, his throat moving as he warned them angrily, afraid to pass them. He nerved himself and slipped down the opposite side of the trunk, pausing, perched on hindlegs and bushy tail, his eyes searching the wood. Shanie and Sandy stood still as shadows and he relaxed, and dug hastily in last year's dead leaves and found an acorn and sat, rotating it between his paws as he ate, spilling crumbs down his waistcoat. He cleaned himself, ears listening intently.

There was a faraway sound in the lane as a car sped by on the main road. The squirrel was gone, up the trunk among the branches deep into the sanctuary of a hole near the top of the tree.

Shanie sighed.

They would have to go in. The sun was losing its warmth and a thin wind niggled.

There were footsteps in the lane.

Shanie grabbed Sandy's hand, fear returning. She had never been a nervous child, but now she saw shadows under the trees, saw faceless men lurking behind the gnarled trunks, heard danger in the rustle of a bird in the dead leaves, and raced at top speed between Cuckoo's home and Sandy's, even though they were not far apart. Sandy wished she had not gone out on Saturday afternoon. She would have heard the noise at the farm and rung the police and might have saved the animals.

No use being sorry for spilt milk. Nothing put it back in the jug.

The footsteps echoed. Shanie wanted to run. Sandy suddenly remembered her father's shotgun. She had no ammunition, but she would get it out of the cupboard. It would be a comfort and maybe a threat. She wished she had it now, loaded, and was shocked at herself for the wish.

The figures came into sight.

'Frankie!' Sandy's relief sounded in her voice. 'I thought . . .'

Frankie didn't need telling what she had thought.

She and Cuckoo had been out, searching for the mare, in the forlorn hope that she might have bolted during the fracas, and not been stolen. The mare was only insured for part of her worth as insurance costs were so high.

Frankie had worried about her continually. She had been afraid of accidents, of a broken leg, of a miscast foal; she had never visualized anything like this. The mare was a sizeable investment, and her former partner was half owner. Frankie felt sick; the loss of the dogs and the cattle was bad enough; this was disaster. She had no idea what Peter would say; and she did not have the money to repay him his half share.

She and Shanie had recently been learning Charlotte Mew's poem, 'The Farmer's Bride', as Shanie had a school teacher who believed in memory training and the child found learning hard. They tried to see who could master the task first.

> Three summers since I chose a maid,
> Too young maybe but more's to do
> At harvest time than bide and woo . . .

There was never time for wooing if you lived on a farm. She sighed, shutting away her worries about the mare.

There had been no sign of the animal. Frankie followed her niece and Sandy into the cottage. The farmer's sister was a tiny woman, lean and hard and capable of doing as much work as a man on the farm. She lived in jodhpurs, snatching a ride on her hunter whenever she had time. Her face was weatherbeaten. Her hands were beautifully groomed, the slender nails painted. Frankie's hands were her pride – slim, elegant, and beautiful, and she always wore gloves to work in. Her dark hair was cut in a short cap framing a fine-boned face in which large brown eyes under black lashes were always the first feature to catch attention.

Sandy opened the door and led the way inside. Frankie knelt on the rug beside the cats and held her hands to the blaze. She wondered if she would ever be warm again. Fear and anger seemed to have a way of chilling to the bone. She shivered as Cuckoo came into the room. Brunie raced to meet him, in spite of the growing kittens inside her. He stroked the soft fur, his mouth relaxing. Anger had knotted him during the last three days so that he could not even eat.

Cuckoo Turpin was a small man, weatherbeaten and bent. Years of working outside had made him look much more than his age. He had earned his nickname long ago when he had written to the *Farmer and Stockbreeder* suggesting the breeding of a cow that yielded only two gallons of milk so that it needn't be milked from Saturday to Monday. He had followed that up with a notion about crossing a long-haired Highland cow with a Jersey bull so that wool, milk and meat could be obtained from the same animal. He was always full of ideas; at the moment he was trying to produce a purple rose for the summer fete at which there was always a flower show, using Sterling Silver as his starting point.

Cuckoo was a good stockman, understanding animals, always knowing when a cow would calve or a mare would foal, and always at hand when small creatures were born, fascinated by the baby and by its mother's devotion. He had not wanted to re-marry after his wife had died. The farm was all his life. Sandy provided him with all the female companionship he needed; he didn't want a woman underfoot. He liked being free to do exactly as he chose. Margaret had been demanding, though one of the best.

Sandy went into the kitchen to prepare tea. Shanie was sitting on the rug in front of the fire, cuddling Liletta, who

15

purred loudly, enjoying attention. Sandy called to the child to come and help lay the tray with scones and cakes and biscuits. She was a splendid and dedicated cook.

Cuckoo picked up the paper that Sandy had left on the table and read the report.

'Let a dog bite a man, or a child, and the press go to town on it,' he said. 'Let men do this sort of thing and it gets a few lines in the paper. They've used up more space about the morals of some little starlet who thinks she's the Queen of Sheba. If they catch the swine, what do they get? a wigging; a fine that doesn't even bother them or that they don't pay; or a few years in jail and a lot of sympathy about bad conditions making them like they are. Human? God must have been joking.'

Frankie couldn't answer. She felt, at the moment, that the men responsible ought to be shot. You didn't let a bad dog breed if you were sane. There was too much talk of freedom. Freedom for whom? For thugs to do as they chose; to break in and destroy; for lunatics to plant bombs that killed people who had no quarrel with them; sheer wanton brutality for no reason at all. And now she was terrified for Shanie, and so were they all, afraid of strangers in the lane who might harm a child as well as injure animals.

Sandy and Shanie came in with the tea tray. Sandy drew the curtains and shut out the dusk. Darkness came early these days. Cuckoo joined them and ate properly for the first time since Saturday. He was not going to let Frankie take her niece home alone; he was going with them. He knew, as he bit into a richly buttered hot scone, that fear had come to stay.

CHAPTER TWO

CROSSLEY PIKE was neither town nor village. Once it had been all village. Attractive but damp and insanitary thatched cottages sprawled along the narrow main road that twisted between fields from Wilston Mannering, three miles away, to the market town of Curston, eleven miles in the opposite direction along the main road linking with the motorway to the North.

The property speculators had moved in. They had razed the old cottages and the little shops and built glass-fronted modern stores; a hypermarket where deep freezes could be stocked and food could be bought in bulk when food was available in bulk; and a variety of office blocks interspersed with high-rise flats which had re-housed many families from the slum area of the big town of Letterton, fifteen miles to the east of Crossley Pike.

Shallow Lane, where the Maddocks farmed, was a world on its own, a part of the old village that was almost cut off, yet was only a few hundred yards from the main part of the new town. It was joined to it by an alleyway that led through the white posts known as 'fat men's miseries' past the enormous new comprehensive school. Sam and Frankie did not like big schools. Shanie was a quiet child who would be lost in a crowd; she needed time to grow; time to mature; and she needed consideration which she certainly could not get among so many.

Sam drove his daughter daily to an excellent small private girls' school, which he could ill afford. But there were only twenty children to a class and the teachers were inspired. Shanie loved school.

There were very few houses in Shallow Lane, and those few were separated from one another by wide fields. The farm stood well back, down its own private track that led off the rutted mud road; Cuckoo Turpin's little house was next door, but next door was separated by three broad fields in which cattle and horses grazed, and pheasants walked regally and where foxes played in the dusk. The house was on Shallow Dene land and went with Cuckoo's job as stockman.

Beyond it, again across a narrow field bordered by a stream, was Sandy's cottage, closer to the main road, and to the big house occupied by Spencer Dayson, the veterinary surgeon, who had known Sandy and her cats for almost twenty years and employed her as nurse to his own patients and as temporary quarters for any strays or problems. She had a big cat chalet in the garden, with its own run, where she could put her visitors, away from her own brood queens. She did not keep a stud cat. He would not be acceptable in the house and Sandy hated caged animals. Nor could he be allowed freedom to roam.

In the opposite direction, on the other side of the lane from the farm, was the inn; a sprawling whitestone building with tiny leaded windows that let little light into the low-ceilinged panelled rooms. A high brick wall hid the inn from the road. Here Sue Taylor, the landlord's wife, housed a collection of animals. She was a farmer's daughter. Her two children, six-year-old Robert and five-year-old Jamie, had inherited her need for beasts.

She kept a Jersey cow and a flock of bantams; store cattle and a brood mare, not so well bred or so valuable as Frankie's mare, but just as treasured. There were muscovy ducks on the pool. Canada geese nested in the field behind the inn and the children were kept away, lest the birds were frightened from their chosen site. She loved to watch them. Often Shanie joined her, and the pair of them forgot both time and the chores, as they stood looking at the courting birds, with their ritual dances and bowing heads.

The news of the trouble at Shallow Dene disturbed Sue immensely. She drove the children to school on the Monday and after tea she nagged them to distraction to stay indoors and not play out of sight. She looked out a dozen times at Floribel, the golden Jersey cow, that provided them with cream and butter and cheese and also provided Sandy's buttermilk. Sandy was teetotal, but she liked the company of her friends, and came in every Friday for her lunch and her special brew. Sue kept it in a large blue jug that Cuckoo had jokingly labelled 'Sandy's Tipple', ornamenting the label with the tiny matchstick animals the two boys loved. On the other side of the jug was a painted cow.

Sandy was a familiar sight in the lane pushing her old sit-up-and-beg bicycle up the little slope to the farm to fetch her eggs. She often coasted home singing lustily as she free-wheeled down the hill again, amazing strangers.

Sandy was a small square woman, square red face and square cut fringe and square shoulders. Her thin straight hair, reddish in colour, had given her her nickname. Her uncompromising blue eyes were set among dense freckles. No one ever found Sandy handsome until she smiled, revealing beautiful even teeth and a perverse sense of humour, able to find a joke in anything, including herself.

She was an incurable optimist, a tremendous enthusiast, always expecting troubles to blow over; the next kittens to be the best she had ever bred; the next post to bring her astonishing news or an offer beyond imagining from a mad millionaire for the latest pick of the newest litter. She was a romantic, loving stories of elegant women and dashing men surmounting terrible obstacles to come together and live happily ever after as a reward for their immense difficulties.

She kept two cutting books: one of pictures of the Queen on her professional engagements, the other of cuttings from the cat magazines about her own winning cats, filled with pictures of feline aristocrats. Like Shanie, she was passionate about animals, ready to take up cudgels for them at any time, so that the pictures were interspersed with cuttings of her own letters to various papers about cat matters.

Spencer Dayson lived in an old Victorian house that his wife hated; the vast rooms were a nightmare to spring-clean and decorate and an even worse nightmare to warm. It stood in large grounds on the corner of the lane, fronting on to the main road. Few people came beyond it, not realizing that the apparently unoccupied rural track that led past his back gate did, in fact, serve as access road to other houses and the inn. Most people approached the inn from the other end of the lane through the fat men's miseries, and did not explore further along the muddy rutted track.

Also visible from the lane was the old Manor House. This now served as headquarters for the offices of a large factory. The grounds proved too formidable to maintain and had been donated to the local Council who had opened them as a park, making a splendid rural walk for those who knew it. The park was thickly planted with trees, the mile-long drive was flanked by rhododendrons, the stream was culverted and led over artificial ledges to form small waterfalls that ended in a lake where mallard floated with farmyard duck, moorhens, two swans and a pair of Canada geese. These all made their nests on the densely thicketed artificial island that had been built to hide the birds from stone-throwing children, the bane of the keepers and gardeners. The Manor was Elizabethan, a graceful black and white building that had been kept in splendid order until the last owner died, leaving no heirs.

The last house in the lane stood in the corner of the Manor grounds and had once been the Manor Farm.

It was known as Tranter's after the last owner, and had been empty for more than twenty years. Ill deeds had been done at Tranter's. Cuckoo often told the story, straight-faced, to newcomers at the Robbers' Roost, his deepset eyes glowing. The tales of old Ben Tranter, who had been a religious fanatic, grew more extravagant at every telling. Ben had been six foot tall, black-bearded, grim faced, an angry man who terrified children who passed his gate. His wife had died mysteriously; his son, a piper in a Highland regiment, had been desperately wounded and come home to die too. Day after day he had piped dirges and sorrowful laments, agonizing the people round him.

Now when the moon was full and dusk fell softly and white mists hazed the fields, glimmering eerily, or when the smoky fog of early autumn masked the woods, the pipes could still be heard, Cuckoo said, playing an endless lament, while footsteps marched along the path and back again, yet there was no one to be seen.

Tranter's made its own legends. Owls roosted in the skeletal barns where mouldering straw hid rats and mice, and stray cats lived richly. Hoot owl and screech owl fed well and reared their young in peace. Only brave men passed Tranter's at night. The children avoided it, scared by the strange noises in the empty rooms. Those on the new housing estates, superstitious, terrified by the night-time churchyards, were even more frightened by the desolate house where holes in the roof gaped to the sky, and weeds, waist-high, filled the forgotten garden.

Beyond Tranter's, grassy fields stretched for more than a mile towards the distant trunk road which linked Manchester with London. Traffic sped towards the junction with the motorway. The main road was invisible in summer, shielded by thickly planted stands of trees, by ranked young firs, and by self-seeded saplings and holly spread by the birds.

The lane had never been surfaced. Cars splashed up it at intervals, annoying Sandy if she were on her bike; Shanie plodded through the mud, arriving home filthy, so that Frankie sometimes wondered if the mountain of washing would ever be less; white socks were the very devil to clean.

Shallow Lane was a community on its own. Cuckoo grew vegetables in his own garden and in Sandy's and shared them with her. Sandy made jam and marmalade and cakes which she sold to the farm and the inn and gave to Cuckoo. Her income was tiny, derived from an inheritance. Cat-breeding was not a profitable occupation so she also crocheted beautiful lacy shawls which were eagerly bought by shops in Letterton.

There had been Maddocks in Shallow Dene since the farmhouse was built three hundred years before. Turpins had always worked for them, a source of pride for Cuckoo. His cottage was relatively modern, a mere one hundred years old; the former building had burned down in 1870, when sparks from a blazing hayrick on the edge of the farm fields had spread to the thatch. Cuckoo's roof was tiled, a matter for regret. He preferred the old ways and thatch was very warm.

Sandy's house had been built at the same time as the new cottage, but the Robbers' Roost was Elizabethan, a place of long traditions. The stone walls were over a foot thick and held the heat in winter and were cool in summer.

On the Tuesday after the vandalism Sue invited Shanie to tea. Frankie and Sam had called in for lunch, unable to bear the farm without the barking of the dogs, without Susie racing to greet them, her long tail wagging, as she danced in ecstasy, overcome with delight at human attention; without the sheepdog always at Sam's heels. Even as he drank his beer he put down a hand. There was no nose to greet him. He had forgotten. Bleak-faced he slammed the glass down on the table and almost broke it.

'Has the lass gone to school?' Jim asked. He was a beaky man, his large nose thrusting from a face that seemed too small for it, his dark crinkled hair standing up from his head in a defiant bush. His eyes were hazel, flecked with green, cat's eyes, Sandy often thought. There was something of the quiet strength of a cat in Jim. There was leashed power in his body; he had been a boxer in his youth and had retired on his winnings, content to live on the memory of splendour rather than go downhill like so many others.

'She came back from Sandy's last night,' Frankie said. 'I sent her to school. She's better occupied. She had to face it sometime.' Her voice was bitter. There was no sign of the mare. She had not yet rung her partner; and she did not know how he would react. She had talked him into letting her have the mare, longing to get back to her former occupation. Shanie was growing up and in time would be independent. Frankie wanted a life of her own again, before it was too late. She brooded into her lager, and left the pie on her plate almost untouched.

'Let the lass come to tea,' Jim said. 'She'll be better with the boys than on her own.'

Shanie came willingly; the silent farm daunted her, and there were too many memories. Her cat had also vanished. She had no idea where Star could have gone. They had seen the grey plush queen wandering forlornly, hunting for her dead kittens for two days and then there had been silence. Shanie had called in vain. Frankie thought the cat must have had some unseen injury and was dead, but she dared not say so.

Sue was determined to make the tea party an occasion. Sandy baked bread and scones and a feather-weight sponge cake filled with jam and cream; there were tiny meringues sprinkled with hundreds and thousands, which Jamie loved, and picked off one by one in the meticulous fashion that annoyed his mother. Shanie barely ate; the girls at school had wanted to know about the vandalism and had probed unthinkingly, asking about the dead animals. In the end she felt so sick she had to go to Matron who diagnosed the cause correctly and set her to tidying cupboards in the sick bay.

Cuckoo, arriving with his own contribution to the party, a plate full of jam doughnuts, at which unlikely dish he excelled, saw Shanie's glum face and scarcely-touched plate of trifle, and began to tease Jamie, who was as mischievous as a nanny goat's kid, and as vocal. He was liable to swop any animal on the farm for any animal that took his fancy and great difficulty had been caused the week before when he gave away the jenny donkey in return for a hamster. Sue sometimes despaired of her younger son. The hamster owner had been justifiably indignant when he discovered the swop was not valid. Jamie was furious when he had to give the hamster back.

'Your dad's bought a bull this afternoon,' Cuckoo said.

'A bull?' Shanie stared at him. 'He always wanted one ... but ... he says they're dangerous.'

'This fellow hasn't the best of temperaments, so you steer clear, or you might find yourself pinned against the wall,' Cuckoo said. 'His name's Hannybull.'

He emphasized the name and Shanie laughed.

'You mean Hannibal,' she said.

'Oh no I don't, Miss Clever,' Cuckoo was pleased to find he had distracted her. He grabbed a piece of paper from the

22

sideboard and began to write, shielding the page with his arm to keep it from Jamie and Robert. He found two crayons and ornamented the page with a border of coloured triangles.

'There,' he said with immense satisfaction.

Shanie read the limerick aloud.

> There once was a farm with a bull,
> The farm stood on the edge of a pool,
> The bull had a name
> That once had some fame,
> As the name of the bull was Hannybull.

'I can write better poetry than that,' Robert said scornfully.

'You do it then,' said Cuckoo.

Robert grabbed the pen and the crayons and Cuckoo winked at Shanie as the small boy, his fair rumpled hair standing on end, put out his tongue and wrote with immense concentration in a sloping spiky print.

Like Cuckoo he decorated the page with coloured triangles, and then, reading through his effort, he marched firmly into the empty bar and stuck the poem up with a drawing-pin beside the notice of a darts match the following week.

Cuckoo and Shanie followed, and Shanie, reading Robert's effort, had to swallow a desire to roar with laughter, while Cuckoo, after one glance, went out into Sue's kitchen, his shoulders heaving and begged her to go and see what her young genius had written.

Sue and Jim stood side by side, not daring to look at one another.

> Hannybull
> Is a new bull
> At Shallow Dene.
> He is full
> Of hay when Cuckoo has fed him.
> He will bellow and keep us awake
> When he wants cows.

Robert stood looking proudly at his handiwork, entranced with his own cleverness.

'Now everyone can read it,' he said proudly.

'It's stupid,' Jamie said, and yelled at the top of his voice when Robert, incensed, pulled his hair. Sue sent them both up to bath and then sat down and laughed until tears came, and Shanie laughed with her. Sue pulled herself together. There was an edge of hysteria in the child's laughter. She took her out to the kitchen where they washed up companionably, discussing the new bull, its breed, and its temper and where Sam would keep it.

Sam, coming in to fetch his daughter, found that she already knew about his new acquisition.

'It sounds a bit of a problem animal,' said Jim, glancing up at the clock. An hour yet to opening time.

'Is it fierce?' Sue asked.

'It's a swine,' Sam said.

'Then why?'

'I want it that way,' Sam answered. 'And no need to broadcast that it's a brute. He's not as bad as Wellington. You remember that old devil my father loved?'

'Wellington damn near killed him, pinning him against the wall of his stall,' Jim said. 'And then you had the Jersey.'

'I learned from them. I can handle this fellow and so can Cuckoo. But don't you dare go near him, my girl. He's not one of your gentle animals. I'm not having any more of those.'

Shanie said nothing. She followed her father outside. He had brought the Land-Rover. She realized when she got in that he had also brought his gun.

'I want a promise,' Sam said, as he negotiated the potholes.

Shanie waited.

'You go nowhere alone, after dark,' Sam said.

It was easy enough to promise. She couldn't go out alone at night. She saw the shadows move, saw clawing hands behind the trees, and heard heavy breathing.

'I promise,' she said. 'Dad, can I have another dog?'

'I've got a pup booked,' Sam said. 'And Spencer's looking for a collie. Damme, I miss that dog; he knew how to bring the cows in without even a signal. I haven't time to train another; and a trained dog's going to cost a bomb.'

He was thinking out loud.

Shanie wished he had chosen a different expression. She

24

jumped out of the Land-Rover and looked across the yard. There was no sign of the bull.

'Where is he?' she asked.

'Safe enough,' Sam said, and as he spoke a loud bellow sounded from across the yard, followed by a restless tramping and the thump of a horn against wood.

CHAPTER THREE

THERE were two policemen at the farm when Shanie went indoors. Sam had gone across the yard to settle the bull for the night. In strange surroundings the animal was extremely unhappy and busy telling the world about his misery. His forlorn bellows followed Shanie indoors.

Frankie had tidied away all signs of violence. The room was almost the same, yet not quite. A log fire blazed in the hearth. The furniture shone. Frankie had scrubbed and had polished, trying to eradicate every mark, every trace, every tiny scratch that might remind them of what had happened. She had filled a big vase with flowers. But there were empty spaces on all the shelves.

Nor could she restore the dogs on the hearthrug or the tiny box with the two motherless kittens. She could not bring back Star. And Timbo, the tomcat, had also vanished.

'There wasn't a sign of the mare,' one of the policemen was saying. 'But we found your tomcat. He was in the field. He's been kicked, but the vet has seen him and says he'll recover. Miss Hilton has him in her spare room. She thought you might not have time to nurse him and she's used to it. She came in with a stray cat while we were there.'

'Timbo's safe,' Shanie said. It was a relief and a triumph but Star was still missing. 'Did you see a grey cat, with fur like those plush toys? She went when . . .'

'She's probably not far away,' one of the men said consolingly. 'It's not easy to get the better of a cat; they're pretty quick to hide.'

'Can I go and see Timbo?' Shanie asked.

'Not now. It's too late,' Frankie said. She didn't want to go out either. She jumped at every sound and had startled the baker that morning by greeting him carrying Sam's un-loaded gun. She was afraid even to cross the yard at night or at early milking; like Shanie, she saw shadows and they threatened her from their hiding places.

She had loved the farm; now the immensity of the place frightened her. There were so many hiding places in the barns; vast unguarded spaces where men might lurk behind a tractor, or behind a partition; might hide in the lofts and leap on her from above; might threaten her with a hayrake; might fire the carefully stored and valuable hay.

She had never felt vulnerable before.

She sent Shanie into the other room to do her homework. The child went reluctantly and drew the curtains to shut out eyes in the night. There was a wind outside, an eerie whining round the corner of the house like an animal in pain, and she thought of Timbo. And hoped, with unusual viciousness, that the cat had scratched his assailant and that the scratch would go septic and the attacker would die.

She hated them with a choking hatred that prevented her from concentrating on her prep.

Three summers since I chose a maid,
Too young maybe but more's to do
At harvest time than bide and woo ...

She closed her eyes and tried to imagine the farmer's bride, the tiny shy girl who was terrified of the big man. Was her mother like that? Little and fragile and frightened? She'd hated the farm, and been afraid of the animals, Frankie had said. Frankie was more like a mother than an aunt. Shanie sometimes felt she should feel unhappy about the mother she had never known but it was difficult to re-alize she had ever existed except for the photograph in her father's bedroom, of himself, younger and much slimmer in unnaturally elegant clothes, and the bride beside him, a total stranger to Shanie, tiny, dark-haired, laughing up at him. People said that she was very like her mother ...

The bull bellowed outside. The wind whined, and a tap sounded on the window.

Shanie raced into the other room.

'There's someone outside,' she said, panic in her voice. 'They knocked on the window.'

26

The two policemen ran.

'It's only a twig of your creeper,' one of them said, a few minutes later coming back into the room. 'Nobody there at all, love.'

'I don't want to be in there alone,' Shanie said.

The policemen left.

Sam had come back into the room. Frankie fetched her account books and sat opposite Shanie, listening to the wind in the yard, hearing inexplicable rustles, sudden swift scurries, soft unusual sounds. If only the dogs were there to guard them; they knew the sounds that were wrong and gave warning. She would have to find another dog; a grown dog; a fierce dog.

Later that night, when Shanie was in bed, she told her thoughts to Sam. He was feeling bitter. The new brood mare had been intended as a thank-you gesture to his sister, to show he appreciated all she had given up for him and the child. Now the intention was ruined.

He was lying back in his big chair, puffing at his pipe, a brooding expression on his face. Shanie hadn't wanted to go up to bed. She wanted to wait until Frankie came too.

'Go on up, love,' Sam said. 'No use being afraid of everything. It's like riding a horse. You have to get on as soon as you fall off. There's things that are sensible to avoid; and things that aren't. Going to bed's not one of the things to avoid, now, is it?'

Shanie thought of the upstairs rooms; big, empty, with hiding places in every one of them. She thought of the lonely stairs; and the sounds in the night. But she went without arguing, knowing that she had to face her terrors and that neither her father nor her aunt could do it for her.

'She could have stayed up, this once,' Frankie said.

'And tomorrow, and the next day. She has to learn,' Sam said heavily, and knocked his pipe out against the edge of the grate.

The bull bellowed again.

The rising wind keened in the branches of the trees in the garden and whined forlornly in the telegraph wires.

Sam was pursuing his own thoughts. He would like another Alsatian and this time no gentle beauty but a dog with a temper. He sighed. That wouldn't do. Dogs bred like that weren't fit to be with children and it went against every

27

instinct that he had. All the same, he'd look for a dog that would guard them.

He suddenly grinned, remembering an incident out of his own past.

'What's funny?' Frankie asked irritably. She had been nerving herself to ring Peter and tell him the brood mare had been stolen, and that within a few days of foaling. The insurance money would bring in £1,000; and where was she to find the other £1,500 that she now owed Peter? How could she have been such a fool as to enter into such an agreement? Her longing for horses had betrayed her.

'What's funny?' she repeated.

Sam had been listening to the noises outside. He felt he needed to make up for the absence of the dogs, by being vigilant himself. They had always had warning of intruders before. The poor dogs had fought, and tried to defend the place. If only he or Cuckoo had stayed at home that afternoon.

'Just remembering Nobby,' he said. 'We could do with him now.'

'We could indeed,' Frankie said.

Nobby had been a brown and white Jack Russell, a famous ratter, and one of the best guards they had ever had. A man from the Ministry had called one day without warning, opened the gate and stopped in horror as a large Alsatian raced towards him, barking frenziedly.

He watched the Alsatian, and a moment later yelled at the top of his voice as fangs buried themselves in his rump. Nobby, approaching from the rear, always ready to defend the farm against intruders, hung from his trousers, and it took all Sam's strength to make the little dog let go. The Ministry man had been extremely angry until it had been pointed out to him that there was a notice on the gate warning him of dogs and he should not have gone into the yard at all, but up the front path, and knocked civilly at the front door.

'I always prided myself on having gentle beasts about,' Sam said. 'And on living decently. Maybe we haven't done right, sending Shanie to a small school. Maybe we'd have done better to let her learn to be rough as the rest, and to know what's what. We don't do her any service by sheltering her from the real world.'

Frankie stood up to put the kettle on for their bedtime

drink. It was early but the room was driving her mad.

'Reality,' she said. 'Why the hell is reality always horrible? Why does she have to grow up and learn that people use crude four-letter words; that they bomb and maim and thieve and rape; that life is real; life is rough, life is not a game? God in Heaven, Sam, how many people do you know? Do I know? How many of them would dream of doing things like this? Why do we endure it? Because of soft-headed dogooders who think you can reform a villain; O.K., you can, some of them; some were unlucky, but there are people born daily into terrible slums who grow up decent. Being poor doesn't make most people vicious; it makes them, very often, much kinder to one another and more understanding. Look at Cuckoo; look at Sandy; neither of them is blessed with riches, and when did they ever complain? They don't have cars or furs or holidays abroad . . .'

She stopped, running out of words and momentarily amused at the thought of Cuckoo in furs.

'We don't seem to be governed by the right people any more,' she said wearily, pouring water on to the cocoa and mixing it until it dissolved.

There was a knock at the door. Sam looked at Frankie and took his gun from the corner.

'It's not loaded?' Frankie said.

'When did I ever leave a loaded gun in the house?' Sam asked irritably as he walked out of the room. He returned a moment later, sheepishly, with Cuckoo.

'I'm hearing spooks tonight,' Cuckoo said. 'Must be the wind. I thought I heard hooves in the lane, but when I came out there was nothing there. Thought it might be the mare.'

'None of the other horses is out?' Frankie asked anxiously. There was her own hunter and Shanie's mare and a pony that belonged to a child who lived in one of the houses on the main road beyond Spencer's home.

'All of them are there,' Cuckoo said. 'I just checked. I brought them in at tea time. Forgot to tell you. Didn't like the idea of them out in the fields at night.'

'I'm surprised you came out alone at night,' Frankie said. It would take an earthquake to get her out there without a dog.

'He's got a cudgel as thick as my arm,' Sam said.

Frankie fetched a third cup and filled it. She had brought some of Sandy's coconut buns and put them on a plate, making the action last as long as possible, needing to be busy, unable to settle at all.

Cuckoo took his cup. The room was empty enough without the dogs, and the empty display cabinet made it even worse. There had been silver cups there won by Sam's father for his cattle, won by Sam himself; won by Frankie for riding and jumping; and there had been Shanie's christening cup, which was a family heirloom, and had been handed down to the eldest child for five generations. It was insured, but how did you replace tradition?

'I'd like to put out that mantrap that's in the barn,' Sam said. The more he brooded, the more his thoughts turned to vengeance.

'We're all changing,' Frankie said. Her cocoa tasted foul. 'None of us would ever have thought of defending ourselves before; and now ... that bull ... you'd sworn never to have another, Sam.'

'Where's the choice?' Sam asked. 'Turn the other cheek? What good does that do, except make them laugh? It's the survival of the fittest today; make no mistake about that and if being as ruthless as the next man is what's needed, then I'm not sitting back and being soft.'

'There's ways,' Cuckoo said. 'You don't have to be tough; just cleverer than the next man.'

'Against violence?' Frankie asked.

'There's ways,' Cuckoo said. 'There's times you have to stand up and fight; there's times you protect yourself in every way you know how. Locks and bars and taking care and not going out; and hiding things.'

'What way's that to live?' Frankie asked.

No one answered her. A diesel train hooted, far away; a lorry changed gear at the end of the lane, its engine noise blown towards them on the wind. The bull bellowed, loud and long and sorrowful, wanting to be back in his familiar surroundings, on the farm where he had been bred, and not there, amongst strangers, in a strange place. He tramped the straw and thumped his horn against the wooden door again.

A cow answered him.

That at least was familiar and he called to her.

'Stir the herd up that will. Be a nice change for them after A.I.,' Cuckoo said. 'I like a bull about the place. I never did like test-tube babies. Unnatural.'

He drained his cup and took another of Sandy's buns.

'Good job I never was tempted to marry Sandy,' he said. 'I'd be round as a butterball by now; never can resist her cooking.'

'Nor can she.' Frankie stacked the cups and saucers and put them in the sink. The flickering fire was dying, and shadows moved in the corners, as Sam had switched off the main light. Frankie switched it on again.

She wanted to be able to see. To be sure there was no one standing in the corners, or lurking in the shadows. She went to bed, but not to sleep, and at midnight got up to check the bolts and bars and windows, and met Sam on his way to do the same thing.

'Leaves a taste,' Sam said, as she went back upstairs.

It was a very long time before either of them fell asleep.

CHAPTER FOUR

NOTHING was normal that weekend. Sandy telephoned just as Shanie arrived home to ask if the child could come and help her look for Brunetta, who was missing. And her litter was due. She might have run off because Timbo was there. Brunetta hated changes. Timbo hadn't moved from his box. Spencer wasn't over-sure that the tomcat would live, but his mere presence in the house upset the Siamese.

Cuckoo escorted Shanie down the lane. He carried a hammer, ostensibly to lend to Sandy, but he took it away again when he went.

Sandy was hunting through the garden, looking under the bushes, calling over and over again. She didn't voice her main fear which was that the vandals had noticed the cat sitting in the window and come back later and taken her, or killed her. It was a fear that occurred to Shanie too. As she looked for Brunetta she also hunted for Star. She had never dreamed that it was possible to be so miserable. When a man passed the end of the garden, and nodded to Sandy, Shanie raced indoors, her heart thumping uncontrollably.

'It's all right, love,' Sandy said, coming in after her. 'It's only the man from the grocery store on the corner. He wouldn't hurt anyone.'

'How do you know?' Shanie asked. She had lain awake from six o'clock that morning, worrying about the people she did know. Suppose Cuckoo had gone mad? Or even Jim Taylor? How did you know that even the people you loved were safe? That they didn't wear two faces, and break out like Dr. Jekyll and Mr. Hyde? She had recently read the story and it had appalled her. Suppose her father were like that? Or her teacher?

'Oh love, love,' Sandy said helplessly. Events had got out of hand, and you couldn't even offer consolation. There was no smoothing over the ugliness. It was there, raw and brutal, and the child had somehow to survive.

There was no sign of Brunetta. The cat was a champion; had been Best in Show and had more prizes than any other cat that Sandy had ever bred. This was her first litter, and it was of immense importance. The kittens were worth fifty pounds apiece. Sandy knew it would be the best litter she had ever had. She had hunted through the house, almost taking the place apart but there was no sign of the cat.

They began to search again. Cats could hide in the smallest space and do the silliest things. Sandy pushed the broom up the two chimneys. Chairs were pulled aside, the settee was moved, and all the beds. Shanie emptied the airing cupboard and felt behind the tank. The cottage began to look as if it too had been ransacked. Sandy shifted her typewriter case and looked behind it, under the desk; opened the breadbin and the deep freeze and the refrigerator; they moved cushions and opened drawers and boxes and Shanie peered into the depths of the drain pipe umbrella stand and found two toffee papers and a catnip mouse and a load of fluff but nothing else.

'She must be outside,' Sandy said unhappily.

It was pouring with rain, the sky grey and desolate, the trees dripping drearily in the wood. The afternoon was chill. Kittens born outside would stand little chance. The lane was deserted.

'Perhaps she's in the wood,' Shanie said.

'I don't know. Animals are funny with their first litters. And there's a vixen in the wood. She might well take the kittens. Or Brunetta might be upset when they are born if she's alone and eat them.'

Shanie was walking down the path. Sandy followed hastily, not wanting the child in the wood, alone. She closed the rickety little wooden gate that Cuckoo had promised, time and again, to mend for her, crossed the lane, and ducked under the wire fence that protected the little wood. There was no more than twopennyworth of it, a few yards of trees and banks and the tiny stream where the mallards brought their young each year to get them away from the bullying drakes who chased the ducklings mercilessly and sometimes attacked and injured them.

'Brunie . . .' Sandy called. 'Bru, Bru, Bru . . .'

'Listen,' Shanie said.

There was a soft faint yowl from deep in a thicket. Sandy raced forward as Shanie knelt to look. Rain dripped on both of them. Shanie shivered. It was cold. Brunetta was lying under the tangled branches. Beside her, already sucking, was a newborn kitten, its white body clean from its mother's ministrations. The cat's dark mask was badly scratched, her ear was torn and her paw was bleeding but it made no difference to her mothering. She was obviously devoted already. She lifted her head and wailed at Sandy.

Sandy bent down and lifted the cat and kitten very gently, tucking the kitten into the bodice of her dress, out of the rain.

'Let's run in, love, and you can ring Spencer and get him to come. She's soaking wet and there are more kittens and she's hurt. It's a good job we found her.'

'I can run down the lane. It'd be quicker,' Shanie said.

'No. We'll phone. I need you to help me; to find the towels and get the heat on while I get Brunie dry and cleaned up.'

She didn't want the child out of her sight. And were those cuts and scratches due to an animal or to humans? Sandy didn't know. She only knew she wasn't taking the smallest risk.

They went indoors. Shanie had seen the vixen's rusty back as they left the wood. The animal was slipping between the trees, as heavily in cub as Susie had been in whelp. Tears pricked again. The telephone bell was ringing in Spencer's home. If only someone would answer. Suppose they were out? It was Sunday. Then the familiar voice spoke and Shanie spilled the story, but even before she had finished Spencer had rung off. Five minutes later his car was at the gate and he was walking swiftly up the drive, his black box in his hand.

He examined the cat carefully. Sandy had partly dried her, but her fur was soaked.

'She's been fighting a stoat or another cat,' Spencer said. He looked at Sandy, knowing from her expression that she had been as anxious as he, lest it was humans again that had caused this particular mini-disaster. It was going to mean the kittens needed the greatest care, and the mother cat. And it was going to be expensive in vet bills and in fuel as the room was chilly. Sandy turned up the heat.

'She should be all right,' Spencer said. 'I'll look in later. There are at least two more kittens there, but they should come without trouble. I'll just look at Timbo.'

Shanie followed him into the other room and stood beside him. Tim greeted her with a small affectionate yowl. He often slept on Shanie's bed, finding his way there up the porch clematis, over the roof and in at her bedroom window. Frankie had moved her niece's furniture that day to a room at the back of the house, and Shanie suddenly realized why. Anyone could climb the roof if Timbo could. Perhaps just for a night or two she could sleep in the same room as Frankie. The house seemed inimical, with new discoveries to be made every minute. Her money box had gone from her bedroom, and Frankie's cheque book out of the bedside-table drawer and Sam's dress studs and cufflinks that he never wore, that his wife had given him for a wedding present. Her own coral necklace had vanished, and the cup she had won with Kelpie, her pony, in a jumping competition three years before. It was difficult to know where to look; they made each discovery singly, looking for something else.

She sighed deeply.

Spencer glanced up at her, and swore mentally. Poor bloody little kid. Life was damned unfair.

'Timbo will be all right,' he said. 'He's a very strong cat. I should think he probably put up a fight. I wouldn't like to kick him.'

'I hope he scratched them. I hope the scratches go septic and they die,' Shanie said. 'I hope they hurt.'

No use saying don't be vindictive. Why shouldn't she be? Why shouldn't she feel passionate about cruelty? As soon as she was told to reason and to make excuses, then cruelty would continue. You could always make excuses. Spencer

34

saw too much cruelty in his daily round; dogs maltreated, cats with airgun pellets in them. He had spayed a bitch only recently because of a tumour in her uterus and discovered it had grown round shot that her owner had never even known about. The fur had covered the entry wound, and the bitch had been mysteriously off her food for no apparent reason and then recovered.

He injected Timbo, dressed his injuries again and stroked the cat gently.

'He can come home as soon as your aunt has more time on her hands,' Spencer said. 'He's going to need nursing and careful feeding; glucose and water is all he can take now.'

Shanie said nothing. She followed Spencer into the next room, where Brunetta was cleaning up another kitten.

'I wonder if that's the only one she had in the wood,' Sandy said thoughtfully. 'If it was a stoat . . .' she didn't finish. Fifty pounds down the drain. There was always something. And with a start like this these three might not live.

She looked up at Spencer, hoping for reassurance. He was good at reading minds. He looked back at her, his face sombre.

'You'll have to wait and see,' he said. 'It could go either way.'

The room was stifling. Sandy settled the cat in her basket. Shanie stayed on the far side of the room, knowing that no animal should ever be disturbed while giving birth, or for several days afterwards.

'I'll drive Shanie home,' Spencer said. 'Can you cope with Timbo, or shall I take him to my wife?'

'I can cope,' Sandy said, but her mind was on Brunetta, not on what she was saying, and she did not turn her head as they went out of the room.

'I'm looking out for a new dog for your father,' Spencer said, as he reversed the car into the narrow gateway and turned towards Shallow Dene. 'I think I've found one. I can't come in, as we have visitors. Can you tell your Dad to ring me? The dog is a year old, already trained to sheep and will work cattle. Working collie, and I know the breeder. Nothing to worry about there. Good sound stock and no danger of bad hips or blindness.'

Shanie nodded. She knew more than many breeders about sound stock, as both Sam and Frankie were fanatics. No mare or cow was ever bred without immense research into not only the pedigrees of both parents, but into their progeny. Sam travelled miles looking at calves from the bull he had selected, and Frankie went to every show to see what sort of foals the stallion produced.

Spencer bent and kissed Shanie gently on top of her head as she got out of the car. He had known her since she was born. She was a frequent visitor at their home. He and his wife were childless to their immense regret. Shanie was their goddaughter.

'I'll find you a puppy in a million to replace Susie,' he promised.

'Do you think they'd let me take it to school so that it wasn't ever alone?' Shanie asked.

'We'll see,' Spencer said.

He watched her walk indoors, and turned and accelerated down the lane, aware that he too was capable of murder. And also aware that the visitors had ridden past his house and that he not only had animals of his own but a hospital full of other people's animals.

And they were all vulnerable.

He was so long outside that his wife came out to see what he was doing.

'Wondering how we can safeguard the hospital,' he said. 'I'm bringing all our patients indoors tonight.'

Sally Spencer looked at him.

'And the donkey and the horse?' she asked.

And then remembered.

'Is there any sign of Frankie's mare?'

Spencer shook his head, and went out to the stable that served as a sick bay, and began to bring the cages and hutches into the house. His brother and his wife came out to help, but there was nothing they could do about Patty the donkey or about old Mac, the Shire horse, who had been left to them in a client's will to be kept in comfort for the remainder of his life.

Spencer locked up. The darkness had never seemed so dark. The night had never been so silent. And then, as they ate, they heard a sound. Bagpipes, drifting down the lane, playing a lament. Spencer ran outside. There was nothing to be seen and no one near. Only the skirl, a ghost sound, dying, and then silence except for the wind in the rustling trees.

CHAPTER FIVE

STAR was an exceptionally pretty little cat. Her short grey fur was plushlike, thick and velvety. Tiger stripes marked her face; her tail and her ears were dark. Frankie thought the cat might have some Siamese blood as her mew was harsher than most non-pedigree cats, though it was nothing like Sandy's cats' vocal yowls.

Star had watched from a hiding place in the straw as the motor cycles roared up the lane. The four men were lucky, as no one at all was about to see them. The farm stood on its own; the Robbers' Roost was closed. Jim and Sue had taken the boys to buy them new shoes. Cuckoo and Sam were both away for the afternoon, not due to meet till five for milking. Shanie, deep in the wood, had heard the noise of the engines but thought they were on the main road. Spencer and his wife had also been out. There were few people ever at home on a Saturday afternoon. Sandy had been doing her weekend shopping, and visiting a friend who also bred cats at the other end of Crossley Pike.

Star heard the dogs scream, and crept into deeper cover. Her own kittens were in a nest at the edge of the hay and soon discovered. She raced out to attack the young man who found them, drawing blood.

He kicked, catching her on the side, so that she spun into the straw. As soon as she drew breath again, she bolted, out through the hole in the back of the barn, to hide deep in long grass, never moving, never breathing. When the bikes roared away, she slipped back to find her kittens hanging, swinging dead.

She could not believe it. She stayed with Shanie for comfort that night but all the next day hunted through the barns. The smell of blood from the calves and the dogs terrified her even more. She raced down the lane, hunting in the long grass, sniffing at holes in the banks and under bushes as if hoping a kitten might suddenly appear there. She hunted forlornly all that weekend and for the two days following. On the Wednesday she left the fields where she had been hiding, afraid of all people now, and slipped down the lane, keeping against the hedge and under cover.

The vixen was in the wood. Star saw her and prudently

37

crossed the brook, jumping clumsily from bank to bank. The kittens were so new that she was not yet used to her un-burdened body. She was swollen with milk, the engorged teats pricking and tingling, the skin beneath them painful. Milk leaked from her as she ran.

The Siamese was lying in the wood, a brand new kitten beside her. Brunie had washed away the birth membrane, had cleaned the baby and was intent on savouring her firstborn. She had slipped out to kit in peace, right away from the smell of Timbo, who even though he was lying without moving in his box, might suddenly come to life and attack her babies. After thousands of years of breeding, Brunie's instincts were deeply embedded, and tomcats were always suspect.

The kitten yawned, flickered an ear and moved, mewing. Its blind head butted against her, just as Star came into sight. Star saw the kitten, heard its hunger cry, and all the passion of motherhood flooded her. She had to have the kitten. She needed it to satisfy her aching teats; she needed it to tuck against her, to lick and caress and to care for. She needed it with a craving that knew no mercy. She leaped on Brunetta.

The cat was taken by surprise. She had been obsessed by the birth pangs, by straining to drive the kitten into the world and then by the strange sensation it engendered as it moved and cried. She had eyes for nothing else.

She roused herself and slashed at Star's face, raking with a savage paw. Star scratched and spat and bit. The wood was wild with the noise of the two cats fighting. If Sandy had been there she would have raced to the rescue but Sandy was shopping.

There was no one to hear the fight.

Brunie slashed and Star slashed back. Whirl of fur and spit and hiss. The newborn kitten lay in the mossy grass, growing cold. A thin wind was beginning. Brunie was distracted by more birth pains. A second kitten was forcing itself from her and would soon be born. Star leaped back and dived on the kitten but before she reached it Brunie was on her again, teeth sinking deep into the grey cat's ear. Star yowled and struck with an open paw, scratching the black mask from the slanting eye to the end of Brunie's nose.

Brunie was at a disadvantage. She was aware of violent pain. She was aware of the need to help the second kitten

38

from under her tail, to mother it and to push it against her to suck. She tried to reach her firstborn, but Star was on guard, protecting it. Brunie rolled on her back and slashed with her hind legs, scraping one of Star's swollen teats.

Star sank her teeth deep into Brunie's paw.

Another birth pain needled. The kitten was almost there. The Siamese was distracted, not knowing which to protect. She was in no state to continue the fight. She backed away as the second kitten fell to the ground. Star pounced, seized Brunie's firstborn and darted swiftly down the lane. She wasn't going back to the farm. She wasn't risking another afternoon with death dealing lunatics who smashed and laughed and swore. She was going to find safety. She curled into a hollow to nurse her stolen baby, before continuing her journey. Footsteps sounded in the lane and she huddled deeper into cover, crouched among tangled dead ferns and new growing bracken shoots. She saw Shanie and Sandy coming into the wood, saw Sandy lift Brunetta and carry her and the kitten away, with Shanie following.

It would be a long time before Star trusted any humans.

She knew where to find sanctuary.

At the end of the lane was Tranter's, empty for years. There were rumours of subsidence under the house, which had become so derelict that it would cost a fortune to restore. The land was riddled with salt mines, which were no longer working.

The overgrown gardens were hiding places for mice and frogs and voles and Star often hunted there, enjoying the jungle wildness, enjoying the chance to hide and stalk and leap and kill. There were young rabbits, and birds of all kinds nesting in the tangled overgrown bushes, in the long-gone-back apple and pear trees, in the twisted crab apples that lined the garden wall.

Star jumped the wall, choosing one of the tumbled places. The bricks had fallen away, making gaps through which the house could be seen, the windows, long ago broken, now boarded over; crossed planks closing the front door; traces of green paint lingering round rotting window frames, giving the place a mildewed air that added to the desolation.

The kitten was warm in her jaws, was moving its paws, was dangling by its scruff, blind-eyed. It was so small that its weight was nothing, not hindering her in the least. She needed to find somewhere quiet, to make herself a dry nest, to savour this baby. To lie with it tucked against her, easing the gorged teats; to wash it and mother it and purr to it as it grew. There were no thoughts in her head; only wild urges and instincts that drove her on.

There were beast tracks in the undergrowth; safe ways where no human could come; fox ways and cat ways, criss-crossed by the paths of tinier creatures; there were little tunnels in the grass, made by mice; harder paths beaten out by hedgehogs as they padded through the night.

Star had used her way many times before, and more than once had sheltered in the cellar in rainstorms. Away from the gratings that shielded windows from which the glass had fallen long ago, the cellars were dry, covered with carpets of dead leaves that had drifted in through the empty gaps. Here, at ground level, the wood had rotted and no one had bothered to replace it. Star jumped through the grating, found herself a dry place in a nest of fallen leaves and there she laid her kitten.

He was strong. He had battled his way into the world eager for birth, and his kidnapping had no effect on him. One mother was as good as another. He had spent only a few minutes with Brunie. He barely smelled of her now. He was soaked in saliva from Star's mouth. She curled around him, blissful, totally relaxed, and finished cleaning him, en-raptured when he flicked an ear and mewed.

She nudged him close to feed. She had enough milk for five kittens, and as his small jaw closed round the teat, she purred loudly, licking at the hard blind-eyed head. She had no intention of appearing again where men might lurk until the kitten had grown. He fed. Star washed him again and when he slept, curled into a tight little ball of soft white fur, she left him briefly and slipped into the garden where she drank from a puddle and returned hastily to guard her treasure.

Danger had sharpened her senses. She was no longer tame. She was wild, trusting no one. She would never again come forward to greet an unknown man.

That night, as Star curled up with her stolen kitten tucked safely against her the vixen gave birth to five cubs; two dogs and three vixens. She washed them and lay with them, nosing each, learning their scent. The earth was secluded, deep in the wood, away from the road, out of range of all the homes in Shallow Lane. The vixen lay quiet. It was her second litter, and she was a devoted and anxious mother.

The vixen could see the world beyond her den. She watched the trees whip their branches across the sky, and watched the storm clouds gather. Beyond her was the familiar river trickle as water plashed over pebbles and under the road that bridged the stream. Above her the wind savaged the trees, their branches creaking. She was untroubled. She knew the wind and water noises and nothing had ever threatened her.

She suckled the cubs all night and left them briefly just before first light in order to hunt. She was very hungry. She drank from the stream and crossed the bank knowing there were young rabbits in the fields, and ducklings on the pool in the park. She slipped through the trees, a swift red flash, the undergrowth as yet too short to hide her.

The men who had raided the farm were young. They all had guns, and they loved to shoot. Close seasons meant nothing to them, and one of them, only seventeen, used his airgun on any creature he saw, whether it was cat or dog, or horse or cow. Spencer was furious at the number of animals he saw each week injured in this way. The striped cat in the first house on the other side of the wood had lost an eye; a child had been thrown and injured when the pony she was riding was hit in the shoulder by an unseen marksman who had vanished from the wood by the time adults realized what had caused the accident. The child had broken an arm. The bolting pony had fallen and broken a leg and had to be shot.

The wood was wonderful territory, right on the edge of the estate that had been built three years ago. They knew the vixen was in cub. They had seen her as they went to shoot rabbits and any birds that flew over; pigeon, magpie, crow, robin, thrush, wren; the bodies of the victims lay beside them, killed for killing's sake. It was amusing to outwit authority, to know that the bikes could take them swiftly away, within minutes. They all had two sets of number plates and basked in a sense of security.

They knew the vixen would whelp soon and when one of them, walking along the edge of the lane, looking for the mare which had bolted in terror, and which he was sure was near the wood, saw the animal run, loose bellied, her teats dragging, he knew the time had come for more amusement.

That night, they brought the dogs. The fierce little Jackie, that would kill the cubs on his own and had worried the cattle at Shallow Dene; the Alsatian crossbred, that Mac had taught to bite and worry, by keeping it for a week in a shed, without any food, slashing at its face with a stick and then putting in a pup they had stolen from its owner a few days before. The dog killed the puppy without any qualms, and Mac, a skeletally thin man whose white face was framed by long greasy dark hair, and fringed with a fluffy beard, had watched, grinning.

They knew how to wait. The vixen slipped away between the trees, to hunt for duck. The wind was unkind to her, blowing her scent to the dogs. She had no idea that anyone lay in the wood. The four men were quiet, their guns beside them. None of them had licences, but it was easy enough to buy a gun and ammunition and anything else if you had the right contacts.

There was a glimmer of moon. Beyond the wood the cottage where Sandy slept was dark; Cuckoo's house was out of sight, hidden behind massed trees; the farm was even further away. No fear of interruption.

The vixen vanished.

There was grey light behind the cloud. The bank was thick with last year's dead leaves, wet and slimed and slippery, so that Mac lost his footing when he stood, and cursed as he fell heavily. They waited, listening, lest the vixen had been alerted and returned. All was still.

They stood in a silent group, the leashed dogs beside them. Mac and his crossbred, Savage, tugging eagerly at the lead. Tich, who was small and blonde with a cherub face that belied his nature. He owned the airgun, and he loved inflicting pain whether human or animal. Even his mother was afraid of him: if she did not give in to him when he asked for money, he would twist her arm until bruises marked it from elbow to wrist. She never dared deny him anything. His father was rarely at home. If he were there, he was too drunk to care what his wife or his son were about.

Tam was also small; he had a squint that had never been corrected and resulted in endless teasing; he had been only too glad to join up with the other three when offered the chance. A gun made him feel whole again, gave him power. He would never use it against men, but animals didn't

42

matter. Who cared about a cat or a dog, or a horse, unless you could sell them for money; and if he could steal a valuable beast he did, and took it to the other end of the country where he sold it to a dealer who never asked questions.

The last of the four was Smithy, a gangling giant, towering above the others. He tended to keep out of sight when they were working together as he was too recognizable, though a stoop helped hide the fact that he was almost six foot six. His family were none of them bright, but Smithy was lowest of all when it came to brains. He was useful to have around as he was immensely strong and would do as he was told. He enjoyed shooting, and could snap a cigarette in two with a single shot at twenty-five yards.

Mac knelt by the earth. He smiled happily. He could hear the soft squeals of the hungry young inside. He snapped the clip off Jackie's lead, and sent it in. It returned four times with a hapless cub in its mouth, which they threw to the crossbred. Mac and Tam and Tich watched, grinning, as the dog worried and tore at the cubs and finally ate them. Mac had made sure it had not been fed for several days. Smithy did not mind a straight shot with a gun; he was not so eager as the others to inflict pain. A quick clean kill, yes, but torment upset him and he walked away.

Cuckoo had been unable to sleep that night; twice he thought he heard the mare whinny and twice looked out and saw nothing. He heard the sound again, and switched on his light. Smithy, on guard at the edge of the wood, aware that the farm milked early, saw the light gleam among the trees, and whistled.

They had no desire to be seen. Discovery would mean jail, and an end to their fun for the time being. It was necessary to be swift and secret and careful. Mac, who had a vivid imagination, saw himself as a daring outlaw, challenging smugly civilized people. It delighted him to read of his own exploits next day in the press, to know that he was operating in secret, unseen, unheard, taking the greatest care to choose a time when no one else was near. The proudest achievement of their career had been the night on which they broke into the pets' corner at the local zoo and destroyed every living animal, so that the beasts were found broken and obviously tortured next day. They had laughed together over the letters in the press. As if they cared, Mac said, though they had to watch out, as Smithy hadn't liked it and he was so stupid he could make trouble. Now Smithy stood on guard and saw nothing. It was safer.

Cuckoo decided to dress. If the mare were about, he might easily find her. He switched on a second light as he went through the bathroom, and then a third as he made his way to the kitchen to brew a quick cup of coffee, and to find his torch. It was not yet light, though dawn was a grey line on the horizon.

Smithy whistled again, shrilly. Three lights meant danger. No need to bother about one. A visit to the bathroom in the night. Someone might have heard them; might soon be about. They would have to be off. Mac grabbed the Jackie as soon as it brought the fourth cub out, brained the cub with a rock that lay near his foot and leashed the cross-bred. Savage snarled and twisted as he fastened the clip. Mac thumped the dog viciously, using his closed fist. It squealed and cowered, and followed him, flat-eared, close at heel, eyes anxious.

Tich whistled and Smithy joined them. They separated at the edge of the wood. Tich took his Jackie, and Mac went off with Savage. Smithy slouched off to the two-roomed flat where he lived with his parents and four brothers. The building had long ago been condemned, but there was no-where else to go. His father had never been able to work for long, as a war injury had left him with blinding headaches that put him to bed for weeks at a time. Smithy sometimes worked, but mostly didn't. He had more than enough money when he claimed social security so why bother? And he could always nick the odd dog and get a fiver for it. And the vivisection people paid well for cats.

The wood was silent. There was blood all round the earth; and the dead body of the fourth cub, flung down beside the entrance, was the first thing the vixen saw. She smelled man and raced for her den, dropping the rabbit she was carrying to eat at her leisure. Stink of man and reek of dog. She sat, her muzzle lifted to the sky and keened, long and eerily, so that Cuckoo, listening, thought of banshees. An endless moaning that continued for five minutes. He wondered what animal was crying. The sound was nothing like the calling scream of the fox and vixen; nor was it like the cub screams when the babies fought one another, called to one another, or bit too hard.

The vixen nosed the dead cub. Desolate, she crept round the earth, intending to desert it for ever.

There was a small whimper. She dived inside.

One of the dog cubs had rolled away from the rest of the litter. Jackie had not found him, as he was tucked behind an outcrop rock. He was cold. The vixen nosed him, and crept to him, checking him from head to tail. He was alive and unharmed. But the earth was no longer safe. The men might come back. She lifted the cub in her jaws and crawled to the mouth of the den, where she dropped the cub between her paws, and lifted her muzzle, smelling the wind.

Only the smell of the morning wood, of wet earth and damp leaves and the blossom on Sandy's garden. A blackbird sang in a nearby bush, a peaceful song, staking his claim to his territory. He would be the first to shout if danger were near. A squirrel sat on a branch near its drey and watched her pass. There were two baby squirrels in the nest, high in the tree. A second squirrel watched from the branch of a hazel bush, its body flattened, only its bright eyes alive.

The vixen slipped off among the trees. There was a white tip to her tail, which had caused Sandy and Shanie and Frankie, who all saw her often, to name her Flash. Sam did not worry overmuch about a fox near the farm. She would not hunt on his territory, he was sure, and she made constant war on the rats round the haystacks in the big field beyond the barns. The vixen made for the coppice, taking the trail that Star had followed the day before.

Flash knew Tranter's too. It was a wonderful hunting ground. No humans ever came near.

The vixen pushed through the tangled grass, holding her last cub close. She jumped through the grating that led to the cellar. Star heard the tell-tale pad of paws, and the thump as the vixen landed, and smelled the fox reek, a musky tang that flooded the air. She lifted her own small trophy and fled soft-footed through a narrow hole in the brickwork, stepping delicately through dust and drifting leaves into the back cellar. Here she found a deep embrasure where she settled herself again behind a pile of stacked wood that Ben Tranter had brought to repair the house, and had never got round to using. Flash smelled cat, but she did not worry. She was preoccupied.

The vixen curled herself on the leaves, gentling the cub.

She was full of milk, and anxious for relief. The cat listened to the sounds; to faint grunts and soft whines, to a throat noise that might have been a purring. Star did not want to tangle with the vixen, or to have her kitten harmed. She knew she could come and go from another grating at the other side of the house. She would never need to enter the main part. She curled at last, succumbing to a half sleep, ears alert, and the Siamese kitten suckled busily. Only yards away Flash suckled her single living cub.

Far away, on the other side of Crossley Pike, Smithy was lying on his unmade bed. He knew that the other three had a low opinion of him. He would go out and kill the vixen, his way, with a clean shot, and he would bring her body and show it to them and then they would accept him fully as worthy of being included in everything they did. Maybe if he showed them how easy it was they'd let him do the killing; quick and clean. He didn't like blood.

He brooded, planning.

He would get the vixen, soon.

CHAPTER SIX

Nobody realized there had been a fifth man at Shallow Dene that Saturday afternoon. Ken Grant had seen Vayla, the mare, when she went to the stud farm to be covered, and had found out her home address from one of the stud grooms. Ken dealt in horses. Sold at the other end of the country, to someone who would ask no questions, there would be a market for her foals abroad.

Ken dealt in other things too. Tich and Tam and Smithy and Mac liked to dream. They bought their dreams; sometimes in the shape of cigarettes, sometimes in little pills in little boxes. In return for their dreams, Ken could call on them at any time at all, and that afternoon he had called on them to provide distraction.

He had not intended that the distraction should be so vicious but from the start things had gone wrong. The lads were high on drugs. They knew that the farm was empty on

46

a Saturday afternoon. They had not bargained on the dogs. Shep, seeing intruders, had flown to attack and the four had smashed at the dog in self-defence with the only weapons they had.

Ken opened the stable door. Susie leaped at him, and as he slashed at her with the flick-knife that he always carried, the mare, terrified by the din, crashed out of the stable, out of the yard, down the lane and vanished.

Fury at losing her sent Ken berserk. He struck at the dogs, over and over again, and Tam, always eager to hurt, had joined in gleefully.

When it was over, Ken crossed the fields, looking for the mare. He could not see her. He drove away in the horse box, which was parked on the main road, well out of sight of the lane, and vowed he would come back again. Next time, he would be successful. She was worth a small fortune and she was in foal. He'd get both animals.

The mare was gentle and used to kindness. Panic sent her speeding down the lane, on to the main road, and through a wood on the other side of the road to stand at last, panting, head hanging, outside a house where the owner recognized her.

He had often seen her in the field. He formed a noose with his clothes line and led her out, and up the lane. He put her into her usual field some distance away, and closed the gate. He did not realize that anything was wrong.

There were noises at the farm; police cars coming and going; a van, and a police dog; and the scent of fear. Vayla panicked again as the police dog tracked across the end of her field. She bolted, head down, and shouldered through the hedge into the field behind Cuckoo's house.

This part of the farm was an elf field. Cuckoo had named it because no one worked it. He swore it was fairy ground. He had a fund of superstitions that fascinated Shanie. There were bright toadstools under the trees; there was a grey standing-stone and a circle of stunted oaks.

The field had never been cut. The grass was high, interspersed with thistles and sorrel. There were rocky outcrops and a ring of high hedges that formed a natural maze. The mare went to shelter, hiding herself in terror, and no one realized how near she was to home.

The field sloped. The steep ridge at the edge of the mazed hedges dipped swiftly to a broken drystone wall, beyond

47

which was the brook that ran through Shanie's wood. It rained all night and the ground was slippery.

The gallop had ensured that the foal would be born early. It was born quickly and easily, at the top of the ridge, behind a hedge that kept away the wind. But the ground was so steep that as the foal dropped, it rolled, hit the wall and rolled again, over the wall and into the flooding ditch.

The mare whinnied, high and loud and clear.

Cuckoo had first heard her faintly before the birth. It could have been the hunter or Kelpie calling. This was loud. He pinpointed the sound, and raced out of his house, stumbling in the half-light down the steps into the back garden where he grew food for himself and for Sandy. He called. The mare heard the familiar voice and answered. She could not see her foal. It was her third foal and she knew it was born; she blundered down the little hill, and shouldered her way to Cuckoo.

He cursed when he saw her.

God knew where she'd dropped the foal, and she apparently didn't know either. Or had she dropped it on the Saturday? Was it dead? Or stolen?

He climbed the fence, tearing his trousers on the thorny hedge that separated his garden from the field. The sun was a glimmer on the horizon. Darkness was easing; the sky was grey and a thin wind shivered the grass.

He did not know where to look.

No use calling Sam. The farmer would be milking. He'd have to manage alone.

The mare followed at Cuckoo's heels. She was slack and full of milk.

The foal was not in the maze of hedges.

It was not in the long grass.

It was not among the brambles.

Cuckoo found the bloodstains on the ground at the top of the little rise. He looked down and saw the broken stems, the trail left by the rolling foal, that ended at the wall.

He swore and ran, sliding downwards, to slip, sitting, to the bottom of the hill, arriving mudstained and soaked. He leaned on the wall and looked into the ditch.

And saw the foal.

Its head was above water and its ears were moving. It was alive.

Cuckoo jumped into the ditch, regardless of the soaking

48

water. He grabbed the small animal, and lifted it, so that he was soon as wet as the foal. He struggled out of the ditch.

The mare followed.

The walk through the garden was endless; the way down the lane had never seemed so long; and he was sure the foal would die, there in his arms, chilled by its immersion so soon after birth.

He turned into the farmyard and yelled to Frankie, who came running, and flung her arms round the mare. She had been so sure that Vayla was either stolen or dead.

'No time for that,' Cuckoo said sharply. 'Look here, Miss Frankie; get towels, quickly, and brandy and get Spencer.'

He went into the stable and laid the foal on the straw. No time to waste. He balled the straw and rubbed, rubbing life into the shivering animal, rubbing strength into its small body, rubbing with all his might, while the mare joined him, and licked endlessly and Frankie came with towels, and they both set to work, discarding one soaking rag after another. Sam, coming into the stable, saw what they were at and went to find an electric fan heater and rig it up to blow at the foal.

'A pretty little filly foal,' Cuckoo said. 'We've got to save her.'

Spencer came, with his bag, with his needles, with his drugs. He examined the foal. Not a bone broken. Somehow it had survived the crash against the wall and the fall into the ditch.

'They're made of indiarubber,' he said.

Shanie came into the stable.

'You forgot breakfast,' she said, and then saw the mare and foal and forgot about food herself as she knelt to look.

'Will she be all right?' she asked. This foal meant so much to them. Even with the farming in its present state, there was still money in horses. Sam had said so, only two days before.

Shanie, listening to her father and her aunt, only half understanding, was often worried almost sick by Sam's pessimism. Soon be bankrupt. God knows what we'll do. She couldn't bear the thought of living in an ordinary house in an ordinary town without any animals. She lay awake at night, worrying lest tomorrow they sold up, as the farm at the other side of the town had sold up. She had gone with Sam to the sale and he had bought a tractor, the whole year's hay and seven calves.

'Couldn't make ends meet,' Sam had said when Shanie asked him why they were selling.

She wished she didn't have to grow up. People died and farms were sold and thugs came and wrecked years of work. She felt very old.

'Will the foal be all right?' she asked again.

And was not in the least surprised by Spencer's answer. She was grown up now.

'I've done all I can, love. Time alone will tell.'

No one would tell her pretty stories any more.

Frankie put her arm around the child as they crossed the yard and Shanie knew her aunt needed comforting as much as she. It was a bleak and unhappy thought.

The vixen rarely left the cellar during the first few days of the cub's life. She almost killed him with mothering, lavishing on him all the attention that she would have given to five cubs. He was cleaned endlessly, and grew swiftly, as she had enough milk for a whole litter. Star also had plenty of milk for her stolen Siamese, and both mothers, anxious not to lose their single babies, were unusually watchful, ears alert for the slightest sound of danger.

There were mice and little birds that fell victim to both cat and fox. Star hid at the sound of footsteps in the lane, crouching deep in the undergrowth, not even her tail or ear twitching till all was quiet again. Like the vixen, she hunted mostly at dusk, when people were few.

By the time the kitten and cub were two weeks old, the vixen was ravenous. Star left the kitten several times at night, ran down the lane to Sandy's home and prowled round Cuckoo's garden, knowing that both put out food for hedgehogs and for birds. The vixen needed much larger prey, wanting a full meal to pack her cramping hungry belly.

The cub and the kitten were open-eyed; the kitten stared solemnly about him; the cub noted his surroundings. Both could sprawl untidily on rubbery legs and could move by swimming across the floor. Both were large for their age; the kitten much bigger than those his real mother suckled at Sandy's house.

The kitten was still white. His ears were growing so that he was now definitely a small cat; he could have been a baby rat before; he already had a Siamese yowl, a sound that puzzled Star at first. She answered his harsh little cry with her own soft mew, that quieted and reassured him. His raucous purr delighted her, so that she echoed it with her own throbbing. The vixen pricked her ears, but did not bother to investigate. The hole through which the cat had crept was too narrow for her to enter, and she had not discovered the other entrance.

On the twenty-third night of the cub's life, a slender slip of light lifted over the trees, shining through the grating. The small animal looked up at it, wondering, curious about the strange objects in this new world that he had not yet found strength to explore. He nosed his mother. She pushed him down and stood, her own nose working. She was hungry and there was a wind, blowing from Shallow Dene, bringing the reek of chicken, mouth-watering, hunger-rousing. She pushed the cub to the floor, warning him to stay still, to freeze, and not to wander, and jumped up through the grating and out into the garden. She slipped eagerly through the undergrowth, following the trail beaten out over many nights by a badger that came to the garden to forage. It was as hard and wide as any made by man on the hills. She side-stepped a rusty plough bedded down in tangled growth, and jumped the wall, padding swiftly down the lane.

It had been raining earlier in the evening. Moonlight gleamed on puddles lying in the cart ruts. Raindrops showered from the hedge as she brushed against the branches, keeping close in shadow.

Smithy had been watching the lane. He knew the vixen had left the earth in the wood, and knew too that she couldn't be far away. He had learned about animals from his uncle, who knew how to poach a trout or salmon, how to call a pheasant and shoot it with a catapult, and never used a gun or dog. He could net a hare on its run at any time. Smithy's family fed very well. And there were always pigeons.

Smithy knew the other three were turning against him. He visited, and they were not at home. Not one of them. He hated being left out. He would show them. He would kill the fox and they would see how brave he was.

He hid behind the trees at the end of the lane. Sooner or later the fox would pass. He had abandoned the airgun for a rifle that Tich had come by, no one quite knew how. Tich had hidden it in Smithy's shed. His own mother was too nosy. Smithy's mother never noticed what went on around

51

her. It was all she could do to shop and cook for the family, and occasionally wash some clothes.

The vixen was hungry.

She could smell hens.

She slipped along the shadows by the hedge, her nose working continuously. The wind did not warn her that Smithy was there.

He lobbed a stone that fell to the right of her.

She paused, one paw lifted, and turned her head.

The shot spat into the darkness.

Sam heard it, opened his window and bellowed.

Frankie flashed on her light and so did Cuckoo. Sandy lifted the telephone receiver from the instrument beside her bed. Shanie switched on her own light and raced into her aunt's room.

Sam loaded his gun.

He fired into the air. Smithy heard the shot, dropped the rifle and ran, his feet pounding heavily down the lane. He tried to cut through the wood, but he stumbled over roots and could not see.

Terror blinded him.

He was no longer even half human. He was a beast, panic-stricken, running from the hunting mob. He was a fox on the run. He was racing for sanctuary, his breath an ache in his ribs, a tear in his throat, animal whines coming from his lips. Never sharp-witted, he was now almost senseless.

He stumbled back through the fence and into the lane just as the police car sped round the corner by Spencer Dayson's house. Smithy covered his eyes to hide from the blinding light and shook with searing sobs.

Sam reached the car. He was wearing nothing but his pyjama trousers and carrying both the rifle and the gun.

He stared at Smithy, who did not dare look back.

'Do you think he was one of them?' Sam asked. He felt sick. Suppose the idiot had shot at the child. Suppose they laid in wait for Shanie when she came out of school. What were they after?

'Soon find out,' one of the policemen said. 'We have some fingerprints. Come on, you.'

They pushed Smithy into the car. He was too unnerved to fight. He wished he had stayed with Tich and Tam and Mac. They never got caught. They would have taken care of him. Suppose the coppers tortured him to make him talk?

Suppose he told them about the other three? He couldn't ever tell them about Ken. Ken might kill him.

He sat shivering in the back of the police car. The man beside him rapidly realized that Smithy was only half there. And not for the first time, wished he had chosen some other job.

Shanie and Frankie were kneeling beside the vixen. She was dead. Smithy had killed clean.

'She had milk,' Shanie said forlornly. 'Where do you think the cubs are?'

She stroked the soft red fur, feeling pity for the animal. Sam watched his daughter, half glad the beast was dead. A vixen with cubs could create havoc among the hens. He and Frankie had often hunted, but he never liked the kill. Only enjoyed the run, the exercise for the horses, and took care to fall behind and go another way home before the hounds packed on the fleeing fox. He had never let Shanie hunt, saying it was too dangerous with so much traffic around. But he didn't want the child blooded. She would lash out in temper at the cruelty she hated. She would never hold her tongue.

Sam sighed, as Shanie stood up, looking down at the dead fox, all her feelings in her face. She was going to find life rough. But he wouldn't have her different.

Up the lane, at Tranter's, the orphaned cub cried for his mother. He was cold and hungry and very lonely.

Star listened uneasily as she nursed the Siamese kitten. She was hungry too.

CHAPTER SEVEN

THE fox cub's crying worried Star.

She listened, waiting for the pad, pad, pad of the vixen along the beaten path, and for the thump of her body as she jumped through the gap and landed on the cellar floor.

Nothing happened.

Time stretched endlessly. The moon slid out of the sky, and the hungry wail grew desperate and forlorn. Star could

53

stand it no longer. She left the kit, and slipped through the hole into the front cellar. The cub was curled in a tight ball, trying to keep himself warm. There was a frosty nip in the air and he missed his mother.

The cat moved to him. He sniffed at her, smelling milk, grabbed at her teat and began to suck, his paws paddling against her sides. Star could not resist him. He woke all her mothering instincts and she curled around him and washed him as he nursed. He drank greedily. His mother had been gone for more than ten hours, and as yet he was very small, and needed frequent feeding.

When he had done, Star washed him as she washed the kit, licking belly and tail, cleaning him when he emptied. He lifted his head to her, needing mothering, needing reassurance, desperate and lonely. She picked him up in her mouth and returned through the hole in the wall to put him beside the little Siamese.

She curled around both as the kitten began to feed, but did not settle. Her half-open eyes were dreamy and she purred, but her ears listened constantly, expecting the vixen to return. She was more comfortable than she had been for days as she had far too much milk for one single kit. The cub was larger than the kit and took plenty from her. She accepted him, as she had accepted the Siamese, and as the days passed and the vixen did not return, he forgot that he had ever had any other mother.

By the time the kitten and the cub were five weeks old, both were well grown. The kitten was a diminutive imp, his small face slant-eyed and wicked. He was mastered by an intense curiosity that worried Star as she was kept busy rescuing him from pieces of dilapidated furniture that he had discovered and managed to climb, but could never come down from by himself. The cellars were full of all kinds of junk.

The cub was almost as large as Star. His small fuzzy body stood on sturdy black legs; his tail was a cat tail, not yet bushed and his games were cat games too. He and the Siamese tried hard to copy Star and wash, licking at the easier parts of their small bodies, but over-balancing when it came to tackling the difficult parts under belly and tail. They compensated by washing one another.

Both were strong. The kitten's blue eyes were eager with mischief. He was beginning to pounce and he played with straws and with strings. He was unafraid of his big foster brother, tapping at an ear, or at the cub's waving tail, and the two wrestled endlessly, chewing at one another. Once the kitten startled both of them by a ferocious growl and the cub learned to hiss.

Star went hunting and brought back small dead mice. These were toys to be carried, not trophies to eat. Each defended his own, growling at the other if it came too close. Star watched the pair of them, a gleam in her eyes, and sometimes, basking in the sunlight that patched the cellar, stretched drowsily and waved her tail so that they could exercise themselves, learning to use paw and eye together, an aid to future hunting.

There were other toys in the cellar. A ping-pong ball that the kitten found in a corner and batted to and fro; it clicked against the walls and there was a scurry as he pounced. There were acorns that rolled enticingly and that were trapped under small gaps, to be pulled out with a questing paw. There were dead leaves, which rustled and might hide endless mice, but somehow never did, although both kitten and cub stirred them endlessly and hopefully.

Star left them frequently. As yet, neither could jump out of the cellar. She brought them mice and small birds, and they fed from her rarely. Her milk was drying up. Rain, blown through the window, puddled on the floor and here they learned to lap.

Both vied to greet the cat when she returned to them, running to her, nosing her, standing on hind legs to pat at her with small paws, pushing one another out of the way. The Siamese invariably reached Star first but the fox cub had more strength and won the shoving game. The kitten, refusing to be thrust aside, slapped the cub with his clawed paw, and swore at him, a vicious Siamese raging that meant business, and provoked him to hiss in return. Within minutes both had forgotten their anger and were curled together in a tight ball of rusty red and grey and black, and white, on which the first faint Siamese markings of seal-black were beginning to show.

The cub was totally catlike, stalking and pouncing like a cat, soft-footed as a cat, moving on paws growing daily more slender. The deep adult colour began to glint in his coat.

The Siamese was growing too, and thinning down. His paws were darkening to match his mask and tail. He was

55

broad-headed, with ears set wide like the cub's. Tiger stripes marked his forehead. The almond-shaped eyes sloped upwards, rimmed with black, and there were pale shadows below his ears and on either side of his cheeks. His small body promised unusual adult elegance.

Star enjoyed the kitten and the cub, joining in their games, fetching both back from too distant a foray through the cellar. The cub was heavy and she had to drag him, but when he protested she cuffed him soundly and he obeyed, allowing her to pull him along by the scruff. The kitten dangled from her jaws, indignant, yelling his protest. His voice was loud and harsh, an astonishingly vigorous voice and sometimes, when he was angry with his foster mother, or had lost himself among the furniture, he cried in tones very like a human baby's.

April rained itself out; May came, with longer evenings and warmer days and bounteous blossom. The overgrown garden hid the cellar opening, allowing light to filter through, so that the two small animals vied for the rare basking places among the patterned freckle of leaves. Star brought them food, and then vanished, and twice Shanie saw the cat in the lane, but could not catch her or entice her.

By now the games were faster and more daring. Swift hunt and chase and pounce and grab; furious mock battles; body melted into body, the kitten raking with his forepaws, twisting free and racing in again, while the cub rolled and snapped and snarled in mimic fury. Ears and tails were twisted and nibbled, sometimes so hard that the victim yowled, loud and anguished.

Then, all energy spent, they curled once more together, the Siamese almost buried in his foster brother's fur.

The cub was one constant questioning curiosity and the kit was as inquisitive. The two voices blended, but the kitten was more vocal, commenting on everything he saw. On the drift of leaves in the cellar, on the whirl of dust in the wind, on the dancing motes in the mysterious sunbeams that proved impossible to catch; both kit and cub tried endlessly, entranced by the elusive shimmer, unable to understand why it proved intangible both to nose and paw.

Shadows were as strange; shadow of last year's dried sorrel head, moving slowly in the wind; shadow of the big tree by the gate, flung at noon, leaves shivering as they blew on the branches; shadow of Star, leaping lightly towards them, her face bent, eager to greet them with a swift lick, followed by a much more comprehensive wash.

Washing was annoyance now. Star needed all her strength to keep the cub still while she attended to the corners of his eyes and the inside of his ears. It was difficult to keep her fosterlings immaculate. Earth had drifted in over the years and the junk was thick with dust and grit. One corner of the cellar was empty and here there was a high heap of blown debris where Star taught the two small animals to empty. The kitten soon learned to dig and cover decently; the cub never learned and Star covered for him and showed him again and again, without result.

The kitten was meticulous and loved digging, scattering soil everywhere, playing for the sheer fun of it in the piled-up grit.

There were always noises at Tranter's now. Sometimes by day, when Star was absent, either hunting for herself, or sleeping away the sunny hours deep in overgrown clumps of catmint, left from long-ago plantings, where she was hidden and snug. Most often the noises came at night, when moonlight filtered through the undergrowth, tantalizing the two small animals, who sat beneath the opening staring up at the glowing round globe, and watched raggle-tag cloud drift mysteriously across the night, occasionally moving to a dry spot to escape the blown wet that rained into the cellar.

On some nights the strange globe ran among the tossing clouds, and they listened to the suck and sigh and sough of the wind in the trees, and heard faraway inexplicable noises; the growl of planes taking off from the airport runways; the snarl and whine of cars and lorries changing gear on the main road, only half a mile away across the fields.

There were other sounds too; the fear-provoking mourn of a hunting owl; the rustle in the grass of hedgehog and vole; the chirr of grasshoppers; the *chik chik chik* of an angry blackbird as a roving fox or a scenting weasel ran by. The nights were busy at Tranter's.

High in the roof a barn owl had his nest. The small animals never saw him as he flew in through the roof, two stories above, but they often heard his call and the cry of his young, begging for food. By now the swallows were back, and at dusk the two watched the glide and sweep and swoop as the fast-flying birds flashed by, hunting the evening swarm of insects.

Star never lacked for food. Voles and mice hid in the grass, and many of them nested. Some she brought home dead; others she carried live and released for cub and kitten to kill. At first they were slow, and she killed for them; soon they too knew how to pounce, and learned about hunting and satisfying hunger. In time they would be alone and dependent on their skill. The cellar gave them endless practice, with crawling beetles and cockroaches and spiders so that when they were tired of playing they amused themselves by solitary stalking.

Frankie sometimes heard strange noises on her way to the sheep, hurrying past Tranter's lest hidden men might haunt the bushes and spring out at her. She often heard yowls and rustles and the sound of crashing metal, as there was a piece of corrugated iron lying on the cellar floor. It had once blocked the grating, but rotted away and fallen inside. Neither animal worried about the noise as they ran across it and if Star came in through that particular entrance she hit the metal with a resounding thump that crashed it against the floor. Often, on one of their mad chases, the cub bounced on to it and off again, so that it drummed twice against the floor and the kitten, smaller and lighter, gave a soft pit pat echo. The chases always ended in a snarling spitting scuffle, a mixture of sounds that were quite unidentifiable to the passer-by.

There were long silences as the two small animals stood side by side, heads poised, listening, and watching. Any bird alighting near the window angered the kitten, so that he chittered with indignation, clattering his milk teeth in mimic fury. The cub was as eager to catch the bird as the cat. Star often hid beyond the window, watching the stones outside, where the birds perched to preen, and the puddle where they bathed, and the dry earth beyond the window in which they hunted endlessly for insects.

But most birds were too wary and her catches were small. Her crouching approach was heralded by an angry chorus, a screech and chuck and scream that meant Cat. The ring-doves in the oak tree were ever watchful, their croons changing note when she appeared. Star could never come or go unseen.

CHAPTER EIGHT

It was lunchtime on a Friday in mid-May, and the Robbers' Roost was crowded. Sue Taylor served egg and chips or pie and chips instead of beef butties on the last day of the working week, and many of the people living in Shallow Lane came for their midday meal.

Sam and Frankie never left the farm together now, so Sam was alone. Careful nursing had revived the foal. It was now a lively little creature, but they weren't taking risks. Sam wasn't sure whether the mare had been the target of the attack. She was the most valuable beast they owned. And the new brood mare, also in foal, as she had been to the stallion months before Sam bought her, was worth a tidy sum.

Sam stretched himself beside the log fire that blazed in the enormous hearth on all but the hottest days. The thick stone walls kept out the summer heat. Little sun penetrated through the leaded windows. Sue had brightened the whitewashed walls with prints of champion bulls, taken from a nineteenth-century book. Sam thought them unlikely-looking beasts with their disproportionately small wickedly horned heads and their vast bodies. He thought of Hannibal who had settled in but needed watching all the time.

It was a long time since he'd kept a bull. The last one had been the little Jersey, a wickedly tempered beast that had tried to horn him. He had escaped by somersaulting into the barn and slamming the door shut. He yelled to Cuckoo, who tried to drive off the brute with a pitchfork. Spencer, coming by at a crucial moment, finding Sam shut in the barn and Cuckoo penned in a corner, had fetched the gun.

Sam put down his hand automatically, reaching for Shep. He still hadn't forgotten the dog. The new collie was due next week. Spencer was going on holiday and had promised to bring it from the farm. Shanie had a young pup; a golden retriever bitch named Peppy.

The puppy was gay; creamy gold with a wicked little face and merry eyes. Shanie never let it out of her sight when she was at home; she took it with her to call on Sandy, who had nursed Brunetta back to health and was busy trying to bring herself to sell the litter. She hated parting with the kittens, always. They were such gorgeous imps. Frankie never left the pup alone either. It went in the car to the shops; and it slept in Shanie's room at night.

All of them were nervous. Sam carried the gun when he went to the morning milking, looking about him lest anyone was hidden in the barns or byres; Frankie refused to go out alone in the dark and Shanie was allowed nowhere unless her father, Spencer or Cuckoo took her. Even at school, sudden panic sometimes assailed her during lessons, a terror that when she got home it would all have happened again.

Sam looked about him, at the black and white tiles laid in a chequered pattern on the floor. At the pinewood benches and tables made by Shepherd Dorton up the lane. At the bar, angled in to the corner of the room, livened by hanging Chianti bottles in their straw cases, by Sue's collection of miniature liqueurs on the shelves behind the counter, gay topped and bright labelled; by the Beswick china Hereford bull, massive, surly, brown and white, his head lowered, his expression amiable compared with the brooding beasts ranged round the walls.

Outside the window a bantam cock crowed lustily, mistaking the time. The sound was followed by a frantic bleating. Sue went out, and those who were regulars at the Roost waited expectantly. Sam looked round him, trying to pick out strange faces. There had been no clues at all as to the culprits. Smithy had been too terrified to give anyone away, and had sworn blind he had never been in the lane until the night he shot the fox. He had touched nothing at the farm and had no part in the destruction or the killing. He had not been seen. The police were suspicious but they had no proof at all. None of the fingerprints belonged to Smithy.

Sam looked across the room as Sandy came in. She always took advantage of Friday to go to the town and shop before calling in at the Roost for lunch. She locked and double-locked, and was still nervous, but she couldn't sit at home without ever leaving. The risk had to be taken. She put the cats in the cupboard under the stairs and shut the door on them, hoping no intruder would look for them. It was warm there and they loved the dark.

Sam grinned when he saw her. She was wearing her best clothes, an unlikely combination of brilliant purple trousers, a white roll-neck jersey, a scarlet waistcoat and a scarlet crochet woollen hat, pulled well down over her ginger hair. Beyond her, Cuckoo, in his Friday lunchtime best, his brown shoes gleaming, was well into his second pint. He had not noticed Sam before. He picked up the tankard and joined Sandy, who was waiting for Sue to bring in her usual glass of buttermilk. Sam drained his bitter and went to fetch another. He stood at the bar, watching a man he had never seen before, who was sitting in a corner, quietly assessing all of them. Uneasiness niggled again. He caught Jim's eye and jerked his head towards the corner. Jim's nod of rejection was barely visible. Jim was uneasy too. Nothing more had happened, but the events were too recent and the newspapers were always reporting similar occurrences.

Cuckoo was thinking. He had had an idea some weeks before, one of his wilder and more hare-brained ideas. He was telling no one what it was, but it might keep the lane private, and the farm unharmed. He'd go to hell and back for Shanie and Miss Frankie and for the boss too. He had vivid memories of the night his wife had died; of Sam sitting beside him from milking time to milking time, saying nothing, doing nothing, puffing at his pipe, just helping by being there while Margaret lay in the next room, and he knew he would never be able to talk to her again. Sam had been through it too. You couldn't ease the pain; but you could be there and take away the sudden searing aloneness.

Cuckoo shook himself. He wasn't a man for brooding. The door swung open and Spencer walked in, bringing a stranger with him. The visitor was a representative for one of the drug firms from whom Spencer bought his supplies. An elegant man, small boned, neat featured, dark hair cut to hang tidily against his head, the gleaming mass brushing against his collar. His lilac shirt toned with the pale grey suit and matched the floral tie.

Beside him Spencer bulked large, his sheepskin coat making him even larger. Though it was May, the weather had changed and there was a bitter wind with the hint of snow in its teeth. Spencer had a mass of shaggy hair that was turning grey and would never lie flat, crowning a forceful face with a thrusting arrogant nose that made many people think him ferocious, though it totally belied his nature.

Spencer collected the plates of egg and chips for himself and his visitor and joined Sandy, who was watching the doorway, a smile on her face.

'John Driffield, Sandy Hilton,' Spencer said formally, old

61

enough to be meticulous about such things. Sandy nodded and turned to the visitor.

'You'll never have seen anything like this in your local,' she said.

The door opened, bringing a wind that chilled legs and faces. Conversation stopped among the regulars as Sue came into the room, and Cuckoo, with a broad beam on his face, picked up a chip and shouted,

'Come on then, little lad, come to Uncle.'

John Driffield watched with amusement, expecting to see a small boy. He was startled when a wild bleat echoed from outside the door and a minute white lamb, black nosed, black kneed, with little neat black hooves, pranced in gaily, trotted across to Cuckoo and took the chip, savouring it delicately on his tongue before he ate it.

'How he survives heaven only knows,' Sue said, as Jim handed her a beer bottle filled with milk, topped by a baby's rubber teat. Cuckoo took it from her, felt it against his hand, then for good measure expelled a few drops of milk on to his palm, while the lamb butted against him in frustration.

Sandy was quietly watching John Driffield's astounded face. By now everyone had left their drinks and come to watch. Bobbity's feeding time was a local institution. The lamb adored the fuss, but just now he was ravenous, and attacked the bottle vigorously, tugging at the teat, swallowing so fast that the milk vanished as if drawn down by a suction pump. The tiny animal was only fifteen days old. The ewe had died giving birth and Sue had been delighted to get another orphan to add to her own growing flock. Bobbity's tail wagged so fast that he sent six chips from Sandy's plate on to the floor. There was a swift scurry as a little collie bitch, till then lying quiet at her owner's heels, flew down the gangway and scoffed them swiftly, and then slunk back, head low, tail between her legs, aware that she had transgressed. She relaxed when everyone laughed, and her owner, a local builder, caressed her ears.

The last dregs of milk went noisily into the lamb's gullet, and as Cuckoo forced the small mouth open and withdrew the teat, Bobbity belched noisily, making everyone grin. Sue took him by the collar and led him outside again, the entertainment over, but he paused beside each man, certain they would stroke him.

'Daft little beast,' Cuckoo said, putting the bottle down

gently on the bar counter. 'Same again all round, Jim,' he added with a grin and came back to tell John Driffield about Tranter's.

'You'll not believe it,' he said, one eye, not on John Driffield, but on the quiet stranger in the corner. 'That house is haunted. Pass it by day or night and you'll hear noises. Moans and shrieks and bangs. Coughs and cries, and rustles and whimpers. And screams.'

He paused for effect and took another long drink. Sam glanced at Sandy, and winked at her, thinking she knew what Cuckoo was up to. He was up to something, that was for sure. He was carried away by his tale.

'It's maybe old Ben, who lived there alone, getting odder and odder. Terrified the kids by rampaging after them, yelling, or threw crab apples at them if they came too close. Never was quite the same after his son died and his wife died. It always was an unlucky house. It was his uncle's house before that – and there was a character.'

'It's above the old salt mines,' Spencer said. 'They stopped working them long ago. I.C.I. work the mines over towards Northwich now and there's no buildings above them. But this place is right above the workings. I reckon some of the creaks and groans are due to it settling.'

'Ah,' Cuckoo said. He had a chip perched on his fork like a pointer, thrusting itself at the listeners. 'But that's not all. At dusk you hear the faraway lilt of bagpipes, soft and low, over the fields, but there's never a man to be seen.'

He paused dramatically and ate some of his chips.

'You mean you've never seen anyone,' John Driffield said.

'No one has,' Sandy said, not adding that the pipes had only started sounding since the vandals came. It was a good idea to embroider the story. The man in the corner was watching them and she felt most uneasy. 'I've heard them three times. I tried to track him on two occasions without any luck.'

'I heard them the other night,' Spencer said. 'I tried too. I took Jackson and Johnson with me.' Jackson and Johnson were two German pointers, amiable dogs with merry temperaments and wildly waving tails. 'I didn't find anyone. As soon as I got to one place and pin-pointed the sound, it stopped and started up somewhere else. It is eerie. The only thing is it doesn't bother the dogs and I'm sure a ghost would scare them silly.'

'Some ghosts don't bother dogs,' Cuckoo said. He always maintained that if you said a thing firmly enough you would be believed even if it wasn't true. Politicians did it all the time. And look at their success. 'It's meant for human ears and it means trouble. He never stopped playing the night my old Dad died, and I heard him again the night my Margaret died.'

Sam glanced at Cuckoo in astonishment as it was the first time he had heard the story, though come to think of it he had heard pipes once or twice in the lane and thought nothing of it. The sound could easily be from Cuckoo's radio or television set, turned up too loud.

'What does he play?' John Driffield asked.

'A lament,' Spencer said.

'He plays this,' Sandy said, and flung back her head and sang. She had wanted to be a concert artiste and had been trained, but her love of cats had won. Money meant very little to Sandy. So long as she and the cats had a roof over their heads and could eat, she was well content.

> Where have all the heroes gone,
> Where are the warriors now?
> Under earth while maids are weeping;
> All their trysts alone are keeping;
> Long dead, now.

'I don't know that one,' John Driffield said.

'Cuckoo does,' Sandy said, half turning her head, and caught Cuckoo's quick wink. So she knew what he was up to. Better not to say aloud. Never tell a secret.

Sandy was sitting facing the man in the corner. Ken Grant had heard there was a second mare at the farm. He knew about the hunter and the pony, but it was the mare that really interested him. He wanted to know about the new mare, but he found himself up against a solidarity that discomfited him. All these people knew one another and he was an outsider. They were polite, but they didn't include him in the conversation. He had walked to the inn past the farm, and looked for the horses. There was no sign of them. Frankie was taking care to keep as much of the stock as she could out of sight. He saw the pup in the yard, and saw Frankie come out and call it. She noticed him, and watched as he walked along the lane. She didn't like strangers about.

64

Sandy knew the man was watching them. It could have been idle interest because he was alone. Or something more sinister. She felt more and more uneasy.

'Time I went home,' she said abruptly. A few moments later her bicycle went past the window, busy purple legs pedalling frantically as she got up speed. Sandy always sang as she rode and the words floated back to them.

'Where have all the heroes gone . . .'

The wind carried the sound away. Bobbity bleated and a dog barked in the lane outside.

'Last orders,' Jim said. Spencer went to the bar for four bitters. Cuckoo had drunk more than usual and was gay. He was busy improvising on the Tranter story for John Driffield. One of the men from the other side of the fat men's miseries was listening, and so was Shepherd Dorton who had been sitting by himself and now came across and joined them. He was a lean man, his face tight and miserable, until you realized that that was due to the long scar down one side of his mouth. His eyes rarely stopped laughing. Shepherd made wood furniture, that was adzed instead of planed, and there had been high demand among those who preferred their possessions made by craftsmen. Nowadays business was bad. No one had spare money any more.

'What's more,' Cuckoo was saying, leaning forward confidentially, his brilliant eyes glowing as he looked at John, 'if you go past Tranter's in broad daylight you hear strange noises. A woman, sobbing, wailing, and then choking to death.'

'I thought she was shot,' Spencer said, suddenly getting the idea. He had time to spare today as Friday was seldom busy. Everyone went shopping, and their sick animals had to wait. His wife would telephone if anyone came into the surgery, but he wasn't expecting more than one or two cases. Later he had visits to do. A horse to see at the other end of Crossley Pike that had an abscess in the hoof, due to a cut from glass; a cow with mastitis at Shallow Dene, but no point in going there till Sam went home.

'Ar,' said Cuckoo, suddenly doing his idiot yokel act. 'But the poor wench didn't die at first; she choked and she gurgled with the bullets in her for hours till her man came home, and he finished her off there and then by throttling her. Mad as a baby that can't find the titty was Jack Hunter then. He was Ben's uncle. It was the moon,' said Cuckoo, fixing John Driffield firmly in his place by gripping his lapel. 'Round as an orange and high in the sky. A Hunter's moon; a madman's moon. There's a madman's moon tonight, and if you come with me up the lane, I'll bet you a tenner you hear sounds and sighs like you never heard before in all your life. By daylight. It's worse at night.'

'Cuckoo, you're soused,' Spencer said.

'On four pints? Not me,' Cuckoo said, wheezing his funny little laugh that always sounded as if he had asthma. 'I bet your friend won't dare come with me.'

The pay telephone in the corner of the room rang suddenly, startling everyone. Jim was collecting glasses, rattling them noisily as he put them on the tray, anxious to point out the time.

'For you, Spencer,' Sue said, wiping her hands on her apron as she spoke. She was a pretty woman, small and dark and plump, with a round face and gentle blue eyes highlighted by matching eye shadow. Jim was a complete contrast, bulky, but very light on his feet.

Spencer spoke briefly.

'Dog run over. Got to go,' he said. 'I'll have to leave you to your own devices, John, but Sally says if you're staying in a local hotel come and eat with us tonight. Hotels aren't much fun.'

'I'd like to, very much,' John said.

'Then you can kill time with me,' Cuckoo said. 'I'll take you up to Tranter's and then we can go home and have a brew of tea at my place.'

John followed Cuckoo out into the yard. Bobbity was skipping in his pen, watched by two of the bantam cocks that seemed to find his antics totally absorbing. A thin chilly sun glittered on their bright feathers. The yard smelled of bullock, and Floribel waited patiently in her field, until milking. She had the jenny donkey beside her, gentle-faced, coat of grey plush neatly fitting, the Christ cross black and vivid. The jenny was in foal.

Cuckoo led the way. He was a dapper little man, always neatly dressed. His father had been a cobbler whose annual birthday and Christmas presents to his son had been, for years, a new handmade pair of dark tan shoes, the leather tooled and patterned and pin-pricked in an intricate maze of decoration. Cuckoo's shoes were his pride, burnished until they shone like a conker, cleaned three times a day. He kept tissues in his pocket to rub off the dust when he arrived at his destination, and now he picked his way delicately between the pools that lay in the potholes, avoiding the thick rutted mud at the side of the road and the heaps of horse dung from the three ponies that belonged to the children at the Robbers' Roost.

John Driffield followed as gingerly.

Tranter's looked more desolate than usual in the thin sun. The draggled garden was full of last year's dead weeds. Memories of ragwort and willowherb, thistle and sorrel, a few brave dandelions growing at the edge of the tumble-down wall, sunbright and vivid against the grey. New growth fought out of the ground. The boarded windows were blind eyes in a gaunt and ugly face, Cuckoo thought. His fancy always flew after a few pints.

They crept up the track through the weeds covering stones that had once formed a path. John Driffield, who was not superstitious, wondered why they were both whispering. The beer he had drunk must have addled his wits. He was being ridiculous. Cuckoo breathed boozily at him.

Inside Tranter's, the cub and the kitten were playing. They were eight and a half weeks old. The kitten was wild as the cub, all hiss and flare of temper if thwarted. His claws were already wicked and if the cub took too many liberties he was well scratched so that he had learned to play gently. Their favourite game was a form of hide-and-seek in the rustling leaves.

The cub had hidden, burrowing deep, lying quiet. He already knew how to freeze effectively, and was able to lie still for much longer than his foster brother. His eyes watched from his hiding place, and his mouth opened in a laughing expression that made him look as if he were actively savouring the game.

The kitten had not only grown strong, but had become even more vocal. His voice would have delighted Sandy as it was one of the most powerful Siamese yowls ever, a deep harsh throaty cry. He was hunting through the cellar, calling continuously to the cub to come out, exclaiming in several different tones as he pounced on likely hiding places and found nothing.

His cries grew more anxious and more agitated. The cub

had vanished. It wasn't there, it wasn't anywhere, and he was all alone. Star was out hunting. She had seen Cuckoo and John, and had hidden herself under the bushes, not trusting either of them. They might steal the cub and the kitten, and she had not yet left them for good. She had a dead mouse beside her that she was bringing home for them.

The cub crouched, revelling in the game even more, listening to the urgent cries. The kitten reached the gap that led to the garden. Perhaps the cub had followed Star. He was too small to jump, but he determined to try. He yowled again, a long-drawn-out demanding noise, urgent for company. When nothing happened, he leaped high, missing the opening by more than six inches, landing with a surprisingly loud crash on the corrugated iron. The cub leaped out, yickering in excitement, and was greeted by a tremendous caterwaul.

'Moses!' John Driffield said, his face paling, as he made hastily for the gate, followed by Cuckoo who was totally unnerved. He had expected that the eerie atmosphere alone would be enough to produce unease, and wind noise and leaf rustles would do the rest. This was more than he had bargained for. Thumps and moans and groans and yells that sounded as if the devil had made his home there. They reached the lane, pursued by yowls and rustles as the two small animals chased one another in the old cellar, merry with excitement at being alive. The cub, delirious with joy, stopped and screamed, the shrill scream of a mating fox, high and thin and unrecognizable because of his youth.

It was more than either Cuckoo or John could stand. Their running feet drummed a tattoo in the lane. Star watched them go and ran to the cellar, greeting her fosterlings with an extravagant mew, and dropped the mouse, watching them fight over it until each had his share and went to a separate corner to feed in peace. Her purrs reverberated as she lay and watched them, lazy-eyed, her paws kneading at the leaves beneath her.

That night, Cuckoo was first in the bar at the Robbers' Roost and the stories of the hauntings grew mightily in the telling.

'I'm telling you,' he said. 'In broad daylight; screams and yells and yowls, and thumps. It's getting worse. There's spirits that won't ever lie still. It means something, I'll tell you.'

'It means you had more than you could carry at lunch-time,' Sue said tartly, refusing to notice Cuckoo's empty glass waving in front of her face.

'I hadn't,' John Driffield said. He and Spencer and Sally had come up for company. There was always talk and laughter in the Robbers' Roost at night. 'I heard it too.'

There was an uneasy silence. Cuckoo was well-known for his yarns, but this was a stranger speaking, a man who was obviously telling the truth and was shaken by the sounds he had heard.

Jim changed the subject, asking what had won the four-thirty and cursing when he heard. The conversation veered in all directions after that, until at half past nine the sound of running feet, pounding down the lane, stopped everyone's tongue.

Shepherd swept through the swing door into the room, his face green.

'Tranter's,' he said. 'I went past, and by Gum, there's something in there all right. Sounded like all hell broke lose. Sue love, give us a double brandy for God's pity; my heart's going fit to kill me.'

Sue gave him the drink. She glanced at him as he took his glass to the fire, and sat close as if he were frozen. Only then did she notice his hands were shaking and he spilled a few drops of his drink as he lifted it. Something had scared him, all right. Tranter's was a funny place, no mistake. She went to wash the glasses, and feed the lamb.

CHAPTER NINE

THE Siamese kitten at Tranter's was growing extremely venturesome. On the Sunday morning after Cuckoo's scare, he decided to explore, discovering a tiny opening into a third cellar, an opening far too small for either Star or the fox cub. This particular part of the house had been used for storage. It led up a flight of stairs to a door into the hall of the deserted house. The door was tightly shut.

The contents of the cellar were fascinating. The kitten

prowled, discovering a battered armchair, the stuffing, damp and mouldy, protruding from the rotten fabric. He thoughtfully raked it with his claws. It tore with a resounding satisfying rip.

There were sheets of wood stacked along one of the walls, bought long ago at an auction, intended for use for repairs of one kind or another. The wood was damp and warped, but there was space behind for the kitten to run along and amuse himself. He discovered a nest of baby mice. It was his first real prey. It was a long time before he returned through the gap. Star seized him and cleaned him. He finished washing himself, and the cub groomed too, exchanging occasional licks as they worked side by side.

The cub was delighted to see his companion again, but the kitten was tired and after a short game the two animals curled together. Star stretched herself in a patch of bright sunlight and slept too.

When the kitten woke he returned to the cranny and crept through, his voice exclaiming as he found an old cheese-press and a meat-safe with a piece of string hanging from the handle, which he teased until he grew tired. The cub called to the kitten, trying to squeeze after him, but he was too big. The kitten jumped on to the edge of an old wicker basket. The basket flipped over and trapped him underneath. He rushed from side to side, screaming. Star, demented by the noise, tried to get her paw through the gap and find him. She was unable to reach him. He ran round and round, moving the basket close to the wall, but was unable to creep from underneath it or to lift it off him. It banged into a pile of cut logs which slipped on top of it, ensuring that he couldn't move it at all. There was no chance of freeing himself. His terrified wails rose to a crescendo. The cub answered and Star ran backwards and forwards, desperate.

Finally, she jumped out of the cellar, heading for the lane, looking for help. She had once alerted Sandy to the plight of one of the Siamese cats, caught by the head in a hole made in the wire of her fence the night before by a fox. Someone walking down the lane had startled the intruder and Sandy hadn't noticed the gap. Star heard the cat crying and ran to Sandy and rubbed against her, begging her to follow. The memory returned and the little cat tracked on purposefully to find help.

It was mid-morning, and Shanie was helping Sandy with

her garden, which was so large that it never seemed to look straight. The child was recovering her confidence. She still had nightmares, screaming wildly in her sleep so that Frankie came running, and Sam woke too, and sat beside her, sending his sister back to bed. It was comforting to lie with her father's solid bulk in the chair beside her bed, keeping her safe. It was lucky, Sam thought grimly during these night-time vigils, that the child didn't know how helpless he felt.

The cat raced out of the hedge, mewing at the top of her voice. No one had seen Star for weeks. Shanie had thought the cat must have been injured too, perhaps from a kick, and gone away to die. Timbo had recovered and was once more chasing rats in the haystacks. He too ran from strangers and hid in the straw.

Shanie exclaimed and Sandy looked up from her tussle with a particularly tough mare's tail. Devil's finger-tips, Cuckoo called them, because the roots went down to hell.

The cat was thin, but looked fit, and was clean and dry. Shanie bent to pick her up, but Star ran, mewing, raced to the gate, and paused, and looked back.

'She wants us to follow her,' Shanie said.

Sandy hastily ran inside, collected her cats, and put them under the stairs. She closed the windows and locked the doors, and added a quick prayer for good measure.

Star was waiting with Shanie at the gate. As Sandy walked down the path the cat ran into the lane, looking back again. She led the way to Tranter's.

'Suppose she did have one last kitten safe?' Shanie said.

Sandy couldn't answer.

She watched the cat dive into the undergrowth and re-appear beside the house. It wasn't easy to follow; the way was barred by thick brambles. Sandy was glad she always wore trousers and the child was wearing jeans.

Then she heard the noise.

There was no mistaking that Siamese yowl. Cuckoo always said that a dog barking would wake the deaf; a Siamese calling would wake the dead. If there were any dead at Tranter's ... Sandy hurriedly stifled the thought. Cuckoo's fancies were addling her wits.

'Do you think Star stole Brunie's kitten?' Shanie asked. She was on her knees, peering in at the cellar opening. The fox cub was below her. He hissed and spat. Shanie lowered herself into the hole and the cub backed away. A cub. A fox cub. But there was no time to consider that now. The kitten's yowls were demented. But where was he?

Star knew where the kitten had gone. She walked to the crack and pawed at it. Shanie peered through and sat back on her heels in dismay. She could never get in there. She crawled outside and Sandy, looking in, guessed there was another way into the cellars, if only they could get into the house. It was quite obvious from the terrified cries and the frantic scufflings that the kitten was trapped. It was also obvious that he had been there for some time, as his voice was faint and hoarse. It sounded more like a baby crying. No wonder the tales about the house had grown so in the last few weeks.

Sandy found the window that led to the part of the cellar where the kitten was trapped. This was boarded up. She found a large stone which she used as a battering ram, terrifying Tich who had been lurking in the lane, and who fled at the uncanny noises. The wood was rotting and the thwacks and thumps were muted and unrecognizable. The crack of breaking wood added to the singing of a rising wind in the telegraph wires. A chance twig, blowing from a tree, completed Tich's demoralization. He had been on his way to see if he could find the horses and also to find out if the farm was still left empty on a Saturday afternoon. They would take guns and shoot the dogs first if so.

The wood cracked open at last.

Sandy helped Shanie climb down into the cellar. It was dark and filthy. She must find the lost kitten. He sounded very strong. He was scrambling under the basket which shook with each movement. Shanie could see it shaking in the dim grey light. She felt her way towards it.

She tripped over something on the floor and fear came back. Suppose there was a dead body in the cellar? But it was only the handle of a broom. She hit her face against the edge of a high chest of drawers. There were all kinds of things down here. Perhaps there was treasure. It made a wonderful hide-out.

The ghost noises must have been made by the cats. The kitten was thundering around making enough noise to terrify ten men.

Shanie reached the basket. She lifted the logs. She moved

them to one side and raised the wicker edge, anxious to see what was making the din.

The kitten had never smelled human before. He had never known anything like Shanie, looming over him, a giantess on enormous legs, bending towards him with long arms threatening him. He aimed a terrified slash at the girl's face. She was able to duck and to keep her eyes from damage but the claws raked along her cheek, scoring deep. She cried out and jumped back.

The kitten fled through the hole in the wall.

He ran so fast that he lost his balance and slid along the floor, hitting a bundle of stacked wood that broke apart. A piece fell on him. He added his outraged cry of pain to the din that the cub was making on seeing his foster brother again. Star settled herself and began to wash the bedraggled object that had appeared through the crevice.

Shanie climbed out.

'He got through a crack,' she said. 'I'll have to block it. He's silly enough to do it again.'

There was plenty of wood. She found a piece of hardboard, stood it against the wall and pushed some of the smaller chairs against it, making sure it was quite flat and there was not the slightest corner through which the kitten could creep again. She looked at the kitten. He was far too wild to touch. They would have to tame him, just as if he were a wild cat. And could they tame him? What happened when cats were born wild and never saw people for weeks afterwards? She simply didn't know.

And was the other animal a fox cub? She hadn't had time to make sure. She was only aware that something else was there. It was light enough to look about her. Star came to greet her, rubbing affectionately against her.

Shanie picked the cat up, delighted to know she was safe.

'She's very versatile,' Sandy said, as Shanie came to the cellar opening. 'She's safe enough here. We'd better not tell anyone about them. Especially about the fox cub. We'll have to tame them both very slowly; you can't hurry it. Then we'll get them out and get Cuckoo to make a very safe cage for the cub. I don't like tame foxes, but he'll be better off there . . .'

There was no need to finish the sentence. Shanie had found the dead cub when she went into the wood with Sandy; she had seen the fox that Smithy had killed. Flash had almost been part of the farm, seen so often, as well-known as the little family of roe deer that sheltered in the woods on the other side of the farm, and that they hoped most desperately would remain unknown to anyone else. Cuckoo had found them one morning when he had been looking for a stray calf, and had taken Shanie back to see them next day. Mother, father and twin fawns, gentle-eyed and dainty-legged.

'Seven for a secret,' Shanie said. 'I knew we'd have a secret.'

She knelt to look again.

'Sandy, aren't they beautiful? No one must ever see us come here. No one. And don't tell Cuckoo. You know what he's like when he's had a few.'

'You make him sound like a desperate drunkard,' Sandy said, laughing. 'His tongue does run away, though. But sometimes that's a good thing. He's woven some wonderful yarns around this place.'

'I heard the piping again last night,' Shanie said uneasily. 'Sandy, suppose it's not Cuckoo.'

'Do you suppose it's a ghost?' Sandy asked.

Shanie knelt back on her heels. The kitten and the cub were curled against the wall, watching her. They did not trust her at all. Both were tense, ready to bolt if she lowered herself into the cellar again. The kitten was as wild as the cub.

'Suppose it's the men who came to the farm, trying to frighten us?' she said. 'Suppose they're using this as a hide-out?'

'They'd have found the animals and killed them, so they aren't,' Sandy said crisply. 'Come on, love, or Sam and Frankie will be worrying. Your Dad's like a sheep that's lost her ewe lamb if you're away too long and small wonder.'

They piled the undergrowth thickly over the cellar opening. Star could come and go without trouble. They crept like criminals, bending low through the brambles, and into the field. Shanie stopped to pick a bunch of wild flowers, to give a reason for their appearance from behind the hedge. She paused at the edge of the lane, looking about her like a small wild animal and Sandy tightened her lips.

'There's no one about,' she said softly. 'Come on, love.'

They reached the farm. Sam was working in the yard. He saw the scratches on Shanie's face, and his heart pounded.

74

Who had done that? Sandy saw his glance and guessed his thoughts.

'She got too close to one of my kittens,' Sandy said. 'It's all right, Sam. Just needs bathing, and some ointment to soothe the pain. Nothing to worry about.'

'Go and help your aunt lay lunch,' Sam said.

Shanie went inside.

'I never thought I'd fuss the child,' Sam said unhappily. 'But every minute she's out of sight I'm scared stupid. Suppose it was some man I had here for haymaking with a grudge against us? You know how much casual labour we used once. It could be anybody. And they might come back. They might be after the horses. I can't sleep at night, hearing noises. I come down and check, and check. And I keep the gun by me.'

'Watch you don't blow your own head off,' Sandy said.

She was anxious to get back.

It was beginning to rain and even in broad daylight the lane seemed an empty place. There was not a soul about. The woods were inimical, the bushes too close to the road for comfort, the trees too thickly planted. The wind soughed in the branches, the wail of a man in pain.

Sandy quickened her steps. It was crazy to be afraid in the middle of the day in full light. But the vandals had come in the afternoon.

She panicked suddenly and began to run and the echo of her own steps followed her. A shadow leaped out of the bushes and she choked back a cry.

It was only Timbo, a mouse in his mouth, on his way home.

CHAPTER TEN

TICH never reached the farm. He dared not confess this to Ken who was waiting for him on the other side of the fat men's miseries. Ken would laugh at tales of ghosts, even though he had heard Cuckoo's story in the Robbers' Roost.

'They always go out on Saturdays,' Tich said.

'They might not want to any more,' Ken said, remembering. He had been angry at the violence once he had regained his own temper, but by then it was too late to stop. The lads were out of hand, and he had set a bad example, impelled by panic. They were always unpredictable, but he couldn't pick and choose. Tich was the easiest to influence, as he liked the goodies that Ken had for sale best of all, and was now unable to do without them. The trouble was, you never quite knew how he'd behave.

'We'll go this afternoon,' Ken said. 'Just you and me. And just to look around. No nonsense, understand?'

Tich understood but he had a score to settle. The scratches from the tomcat had gone septic. If he saw the brute he'd do it in. Otherwise, he'd play ball. You had to, with Ken.

Frankie had taken Shanie shopping. Sam sat in the kitchen cleaning his gun, listening for noises. Cuckoo was about too. Both men were now sure the horses were the target. A car changed gear on the main road, and Sam jumped up and walked nervously to the window.

There were two men by the stable door.

One of them was the man who had been in the Robbers' Roost. So his instinct had been right. The other was much younger, small with an angelic face. Sam knew that type. He'd once sung in the choir himself. He picked up the gun, without loading it, and he walked outside.

'And who the hell are you?' Sam asked, as both men jumped to face him.

'Just looking. I wanted a word,' Ken said.

'You're trespassing,' Sam said. He held the gun against him. 'Get off or I'll shoot.'

'Just wondered if you had a horse for sale,' Tich said hastily and Ken swore under his breath. He could have kicked the fool. Sam's eyes widened.

'I have nothing for sale,' he said.

Cuckoo came round the corner of the barn. He held the pitchfork.

'Trouble?' he asked softly.

'No trouble,' Ken said hastily. 'Just heard you had a horse for sale. Must have been mistaken.'

The two men walked out of the yard and into the lane. Sam watched them go.

76

'You wouldn't have shot?' Cuckoo asked.

'It isn't even loaded. I was cleaning it. The older man was in the Roost. Do you think . . .' He couldn't bring himself to say what he thought.

'No harm in giving the police a description,' Cuckoo said.

'And what will they do?' Sam asked sourly. 'Write it down and say perhaps and if they're not in the Rogues' Gallery how do they pin anything on them? I don't want to have to wait till they try again.'

'What can you do?' Cuckoo asked.

'Send the horses away,' Sam said.

'And suppose they go after Shanie in revenge? They're mad enough,' Cuckoo said, and then was sorry he had voiced his thoughts. Sam stared at him, and his fingers tightened on the gun.

'I'll take care of that,' he said. 'A man's entitled to protect himself, isn't he? Or am I supposed to sit like a knitting Nancy and wait for them to come back? The police won't wait with me. They come afterwards. It's too late then. I'm not putting up with it again, I can tell you.'

'You won't use the gun,' Cuckoo said again.

'I won't use the gun,' Sam answered. He walked across to the stable and opened the door and stood for a very long time, just looking inside.

Down the lane Timbo had finished his mouse. He heard footsteps and recognized them and ran. He raced along the ditch, his small heart thumping uncontrollably, memory wakening terror. He knew the scent of Tich; the scent of shaving lotion and cigarettes and something else beside, dark and fearful, an aura of hatred that reached the cat.

There was an oak tree in the hedge. Timbo climbed swiftly, high into the trunk, startling a squirrel that chittered and lashed its tail. Timbo wasn't hunting, he was hiding. The squirrel vanished and the cat clawed against the tree branch, holding tightly, looking down.

The two heads passed below him.

The fair-haired man laughed and the older man said something in a soft voice.

It was a very long time before the cat climbed down from the tree.

He passed Frankie, driving Shanie home. Frankie was aware that the child was seething with excitement, with some special knowledge of her own.

'Can I go and see Sandy?' Shanie asked, as soon as the car stopped.

'I'll get jealous,' Frankie said. 'What's Sandy got that I haven't got?'

Shanie looked at her. Secrets shouldn't be shared among too many, but Frankie was special.

'Come with me and see,' she said, and leading her aunt along the lane, they stole like two truants through the little wood. The house seemed emptier than ever, creepy and isolated. Shanie was cautious, looking about her. She did not want anyone to see them enter the garden. Frankie followed, curious, stooping through the overhanging branches, slipping silently among the high grass, avoiding thistles and nettles. Tranter's loomed ahead of them, its empty windows black and forbidding, furred with cobwebs, shuttered with planks of wood.

Shanie put a finger to her lips. Star appeared from nowhere, mewing softly, weaving round the child's legs, purring. She rolled, paws curled, and Frankie stroked the soft fur. A blackbird chittered angrily. Cat. Cat. Cat. The cry was echoed and repeated until the garden was alive with rage.

Shanie led her aunt to the cellar opening. The kitten and the cub were curled together, sound asleep. Frankie knelt, seeing the rusty fur, the pricked ears, the tail now beginning to bush; and close against it the slender body of the little Siamese.

The kitten stretched, opened wide blue eyes, and spat. The cub hissed.

The cellar floor was empty; both had vanished, hiding from intruders, wary as any wild creature. Frankie sat back on her heels. So this was the child's secret. The kitten would need to be tamed. And what about the cub? They dared not take it to the farm; not now, when every night was shadowed by fear; not now, when she woke at the cry of the owl, wondering if men lurked outside, waiting to steal, and to hurt.

She had no need for Shanie to impress stealth on her as they crept warily from the bushes and cut across the corner of the field and looked uneasily up and down the lane before slipping through the hedge again.

Back at the farm Sam had finished cleaning his gun. He stood, staring at it, lips compressed, as Frankie and Shanie came into the room.

'We had visitors,' he said, facing his sister. 'Some man that wanted to know if we have a horse for sale. It's the mare they're after, and that foal. Would that partner of yours take the horses? Does anyone know that you were ever associated?'

Frankie walked over to the window. Not even Sam knew of that brief disastrous courtship. Shanie had been four months old, and she couldn't leave them. She had not seen Peter since. They had known each other for years; ridden together in competitions; worked the horses together, and there had been nothing between them until she left the stables to look after her orphaned niece. He was married now. She had spoken on the telephone to him when arranging the arrival of the mare. Now she regretted the whole transaction. Twelve years was a long time.

'Nobody knows,' Frankie said bleakly. 'I'll miss the horses. Damn them to hell,' she added violently and went to look up the phone number in the address book that she kept in her bedside-table drawer. There was a letter there too and a photograph.

She dialled the number, and listened to the voice that answered, and realized afresh that memory still had the power to hurt.

'He'll take them,' she said later. 'We'll have to make arrangements. And they mustn't go from here. Suppose they were followed?'

'They can go at night,' Sam said. 'Spencer has a horse box. Cuckoo and I can walk them down to him when we are sure that no one is about, and I'll get Shepherd to drive them for me. He likes driving, and he's always glad of extra cash. Business isn't as good as it used to be.'

Sam went out to find Shepherd and to contact Spencer, and Frankie watched anxiously, lest any stranger came up the lane. Shanie was playing with the pup. They were tugging together at a rope. She was a gay little animal and had been house-trained in a few short days. The child was already besotted about her and she about Shanie. But they would need another dog to guard the house. Retrievers were too friendly.

There were footsteps in the lane. Frankie went to the window. Shanie lifted the pup and ran indoors, to stand beside her aunt and stare through the glass, as the steps came closer. Timbo had flashed inside, and was already upstairs, in

79

his favourite hiding place behind the hot water cylinder. His green eyes glowed in the dark, and he held his breath. He rarely came down until the house was locked for the night, and he had given up his midnight hunting, preferring the sanctuary of the enclosing walls.

It was only Cuckoo, bringing a present of guinea fowl eggs for Shanie who loved them. Cuckoo had been visiting his brother at the other end of the town.

'We'll all be running from shadows next,' Frankie said lightly, wishing she could relax, and that the child could relax too.

'Shadows don't hurt,' Shanie said, as she filled the pup's waterbowl and watched her drink, and then sat on the hearthrug, holding the bitch close as if she could protect her from all the evil in the world.

Cuckoo looked at them and then looked across the room at Frankie. He tightened his mouth. If he were young again . . . but it was no use regretting. He went outside to check the farm and double-check, testing the doors of the calf pens, now heavily padlocked; and running a light hand over the mare's neck.

She rubbed against his arm.

Overhead, a plane sped across the sky. A drift of seed from the willowherb opposite floated on the wind. Timbo crept downstairs. Cuckoo shut the farm gate behind him and went home.

Two hours later, soft and mournful, came the lilt of the pipes. Dusk hid the hedges and deepened into dark. Sam, coming into the room, stopped to listen, head cocked on one side, and looked at his sister.

'And what the devil is THAT?' he asked.

The notes changed.

The rising wind keened in the wires; a horse stamped uneasily. Sam walked outside.

Nothing moved in the lane.

Only the wind rustled the leaves.

There was silence.

And then the sound of footsteps, and the wail of a lament, played on the bagpipes.

Sam strode to the gate.

Lights blazed in every room in Cuckoo's little house; lights patched the lane and reflected in puddles left by a later shower; lights angled across the farmyard.

The music died on the wind.

Sam went back into the house, to face Shanie's questioning eyes, and Frankie's anxious face.

'There's nobody there,' he said.

CHAPTER ELEVEN

SANDY began to feel that everybody in the lane had secrets. She heard the horses pass her window, late at night, and looked out. Sam was riding the hunter and leading the mare; Cuckoo had the foal on a halter, and also the second mare that Sam had bought, so long ago, and yet so recently. Kelpie followed them. Sandy watched, anxious, lest the shadows hid strangers who might attack. Spencer was keeping the horses hidden. Shepherd would need to make several journeys. Sam had decided all the horses were at risk.

Sandy had locked her doors twice that night, checking again, checking the windows, that now were fitted with screws and keys. Cuckoo had spent the whole of one Sunday fitting them to his windows, to Sandy's windows and to the windows on the farm. He had fitted bolts and padlocks to the stable doors; had thought of burglar alarms and booby traps and had spoken to a friend who worked for an electronics firm to see if he could think of a way of wiring the place so that intruders would set off the alarms and animals wouldn't. That problem proved insoluble.

Sandy took the cats into her bedroom. She slept with the pepper pot on the table beside her bed and a heavy cudgel, red velvet wrapped, that had belonged to her father, a cantankerous old invalid who used it to rap on the floor when he wanted his wife or his daughter. Sandy, who was an inveterate hoarder, was glad she had kept it. She felt safer with it at her bedside and checked to see that it was there when she made the bed.

She wished she could bring Brunie's kitten home; it was quite wild, and would need taming. And the fox cub posed problems. Star had done her best but her diet of mice and birds was not ideal. Sandy visited regularly with plates of food. The cub and the kitten would never come out of hiding while she was there, but they fed as soon as she had gone and with luck they would get used to her smell, which was on the plates.

Life had settled into an uneasy pattern. It was strange without the horses. Sam hated the empty stables. He knew that the child missed the foal which had learned to come like a dog to a whistle and had been a friendly little beast. It was safely settled with the other horses at the other end of the country. Peter had phoned Spencer. Better not to communicate direct. Sam felt as if he were living in a state of siege, a feeling that was intensified the day that Timbo met Tich for a third time in the lane.

Tich was on his motor bike. He saw the cat, and tried to run it down. But Timbo moved fast. He caught the end of his tail under the spinning wheels and leaped free, over the wall, hiding in the thick bushes around the stream. Tich beat through the bushes but never saw the cat. At last he rode on, vowing vengeance. Sandy saw the motor bike, and quickly gathered her cats and put them under the stairs, so that they could not be seen on window-sills or in doorways. She remembered the bikes on the day that the farm had been raided. She had seen them, the four of them, in convoy in the lane.

Mindless monsters in Martian helmets.

Timbo crept out, and ran to Sandy, crying to be let in. The end of his tail was a raw stump. Sandy rang Spencer, who came at once.

'Do you think he did it on purpose?' Sandy asked.

Spencer, who had been operating on a dog run over that morning by another motor bike that, according to a passer-by, had swerved deliberately to hit it, said nothing. He tightened his lips. He hated the town that had encroached on their privacy; hated the men it had brought with it; without heed for animals or for children. He thought of the child that stood in his surgery the day before, tears spilling silently down bruised cheeks, holding in her arms a cat that had been kicked almost to death by her drunken stepfather. He had put the cat down. There was little he could do about the child.

He could rescue animals. How could you start a home for the babies born to those who did not deserve children? He was too angry to answer Sandy, who did not ask questions.

She had been with Spencer one day when he found three boys torturing a kitten. The boys were sore for days, as Spencer put them across his knee and spanked them hard. He had to put the kitten to sleep. He made the boys watch and offered to put them down too if they told the police. They were young enough to believe him and be afraid. If he caught them once more, he said . . .

He was not proud of himself, but what could you do?

The two barns behind his house were full of rescued cats. Cats taken from slum clearance areas; cats 'stolen' by people who knew they were neglected or abused; cats that had been run over, and that nobody had claimed.

Sandy helped with them; helped to rescue them; went round the depressed regions offering children fifty pence for each cat she saw in need of treatment. No one but Spencer knew how she spent her spare time. Every time she sold a litter the money from one kitten went into Spencer's private fund for his rescued animals. There was always a stray to replace a lost pet. Spencer's strays were up at Shallow Dene Farm; were at the Robbers' Roost; Shepherd, now back from driving the horses to safety, had two of them; one was a pedigree white Persian; goodness knew how it had come to be found in the river, in a small bag, weighted down with stones. Two boys fishing for tiddlers saw a man throw the bag away and had gone, curious, to look.

Spencer knew Shanie's secret; but felt it unwise to visit Tranter's himself. Too many people around would draw attention to the place; they would trample the trails, and it would be obvious that there were visitors. It explained the hideous noises; fox cry and Siamese wail were more uncanny than a hunting owl, or the clamorous warning clang of the cock pheasant.

Sam became morose. He was silent, sitting, staring at the wall, and frequently neither heard nor answered when Frankie or Shanie spoke. Frankie herself was depressed, missing the horses more than she believed possible, worried if Shanie was a second late from school, wishing she had not sent her horses to Peter; wondering what she had missed by staying with her brother, giving all her life to him and to her niece. Peter now had children of his own. But there might have been other men.

She had never regretted her life before; now there was too much time to think. And the farm felt so isolated, when Sam and Cuckoo were busy in the fields. She took to keeping the ganders in the yard as watchdogs; they made more noise when strangers came than any of the dogs. The new collie was a silent little creature, leaping out, growling under her breath; and the bitch, Peppy, was a fool, rushing to greet total strangers with something in her mouth; often Frankie's purse, lifted from her handbag. Shanie was beginning to teach her to fetch a rubber dumbbell when she threw it, and the bitch brought it back proudly, carrying her head high, tail waving ecstatically, and delivered it, slimed and wet, into the child's hand.

Smithy had been freed; there was nothing to connect him with the vandals, and killing a fox was not a crime. All the local farmers were apt to shoot them if they found them on their land. Nobody hunted any more; and the cubs grew and bred and there were foxes running through the towns, raiding the bins, keeping down the rats.

Ken continued to visit the Robbers' Roost. He listened, and watched. He had all the time in the world, but he was an outsider, and none of the regulars trusted him. Jim didn't like the man, but a publican had no choice. The stranger was never drunk; he behaved himself perfectly, but there was something about him ...

Sam glowered if Ken were there, and answered abruptly. Once the man had been unwise enough to ask about the horses.

'Sold them,' Sam said. 'Can't make ends meet these days.'

It was a likely enough story but Sam didn't think he was believed.

That night, he spent almost an hour standing in front of the stable that contained the bull. Frankie wanted Hannibal moved to the old bull pen, which was far stronger, as she felt that the stable was too flimsy for the animal.

Sam was adamant. The bull stayed there.

He liked having a bull. A.I. was all very well, but it wasn't the same as breeding your own animals, able to watch the calves develop and pick out their characters, some like their mother and some like their father. The little Jersey bull had had a trick of staring at you with his head on one side, one horn dangerously lowered. It was a trait that he passed on to nearly all his sons.

That had been a tiny bull. Wicked as they come for all that.

Hannibal was a Hereford, his massive face white, with a curly pool of hair between the angled horns. He was immense, short-legged and curly-chested. Sam had bought him cheap; few local farmers wanted beef cattle just now, but Sam hadn't his mind on profit; he wanted the bull about; he wanted him in the farmyard; and he watched approvingly as the animal turned restlessly and drove his horn at the wall.

Sam fastened the rope through the ring and led him outside.

'You're mad,' Frankie said, crossing the yard with a bucket of eggs which needed washing before she could box them.

Sam said nothing.

The bull danced with anger. He lowered his horns at Cuckoo who had just finished feeding the horses and bedding them. Cuckoo dodged deftly. Sam led the bull back into the stable that had belonged to the mare. He never put the animal in the same place twice running. He closed the door and padlocked it.

'I hope to God it's strong enough,' Cuckoo said, as he went.

That night, when Frankie went to bed, she looked out of her bedroom window. Sam was standing by the stable, the half door open, feeding the bull with pony nuts, scratching the fringed head, talking softly to the animal, gentling him.

Bagpipes sounded in the lane.

Sam did not even turn his head.

Frankie heard the front door shut and bolts shoot home, and the music played on, and over and above it came a long eerie scream. A small pyjama-clad figure crept into the room. Frankie turned her head and made room for Shanie to snuggle into the bed. It wasn't the first time since the vandalism and it wouldn't be the last. But at least the child no longer had nightmares.

There was a swift movement and Timbo, leaping through the open window, landed on the eiderdown. He had climbed the creeper and balanced on the sill before jumping. Frankie opened her eyes again.

'Nothing like keeping open house in bed,' she said. But she made no attempt to evict the cat, and, unable to get to sleep, she was glad of the soft purr that throbbed in the room, while outside, in the wood, owls screeched in the rain.

CHAPTER TWELVE

FRANKIE was cooking bacon, listening for unusual noises, and reading the horoscopes in the daily paper, an activity Sam despised openly, although Shanie and her aunt knew he peeped secretly at his when he thought they were not looking. Frankie and Shanie had been born in late May; Gemini described both of them; unpredictable, quick-thinking and impatient, with periods of introspective misery that shattered them and were followed by equally unreasonable periods of high elation. They were either up in the air or down in the depths and life was difficult when their moods failed to coincide.

Sam, Frankie thought, was a typical Taurus, slow, bull-like, obstinate, liking routine, hating anything that disrupted the even tenor of living. And as life under successive governments was never more uncertain and the vandals had added their blows to Sam's peace-loving mind, she worried more and more about her brother. He had none of his daughter's or his sister's resilience. He brooded, worryingly, and seemed to spend more and more time with the bull.

The pup was lying on her back, holding her blue rubber dumbbell between big fluffy paws, juggling it merrily, an entertained look in her eye. Frankie put down the paper and watched. As far as she could see, she and Shanie would do well to go straight back to bed. It was ridiculous to believe in horoscopes, but she always had a sneaking feeling that they might be right. She looked at hers again.

'Peace and quiet will be broken by unnecessary commotion. A bad day for travelling.'

Sam's was even worse.

'You will make an unpleasant discovery to do with your business. The stars are against you for the next two weeks. Someone close to you will have an unpleasant surprise.'

How stupid can you get, Frankie thought crossly, and then pulled out the grill pan. She stared at the bacon, not knowing whether to laugh or cry. She had completely forgotten to keep an eye on it, and each piece was shrivelled black. And there wasn't any more. Oh well, that was Sam's horoscope. She was close to him and she had had an unpleasant surprise. She went to the pantry and found a tin of luncheon meat. She would have to fry it with the eggs and she would have to be quick, daydreaming away, while the ticking clock hurried on without her.

Shanie came racing down and hugged the pup who dropped her dumbbell, and performed an ecstatic dance of adoration, every part of her small sinewy body waggling with delight. Shanie kissed the top of her domed head and hugged her tight.

'You'll be late for school, love,' Frankie said. 'Spencer said he'd take you. He has to go and look at a dog at the house at the end of the school road. He'll be here soon. Eat up, chop chop.'

'Cuckoo's out in the yard,' Shanie said, her mouth full. 'Dad must have gone out to get him. Has something happened?'

'Not as far as I know,' Frankie said. If there'd been any trouble there would have been noises. She couldn't think of any reason why Cuckoo should be early. None of the cows was due to calve.

'Maybe Buffet farrowed,' Shanie said suddenly.

Frankie frowned. She was angry about Buffet. There was swine fever in the area and a standstill order on pigs. None could be bought or sold, or moved from farm to farm. They still had the piglets from the last litter, growing daily and eating enormously. They should have been sold weeks ago. But swine fever was as disastrous as foot and mouth and if you got it all the pigs had to be slaughtered.

Which meant that Buffet couldn't go to the boar at Swallow Hill as she should have done and after a furious argument, Sam had mated Buffet to her own father. Frankie was as horrified as if the sow had been human.

She hated inbreeding, whether cat or dog or cow or horse or pig, convinced that it always brought trouble.

'Father would turn in his grave,' she said at last, in desperation. Jim Maddock would no more have mated the sow to her own father than he would have missed going to church every Sunday morning, an obstinacy that finally killed him, as he walked there on his eighty-fifth birthday, suffering from a heavy cold. There was a national strike and no heating in the church and the cold had turned to pneumonia. Sam was as pigheaded in a different way.

'Father didn't live now. He never had to contend with the things that we endure,' Sam said. 'What do we eat, may I

87

ask? If there aren't any pigs to sell what do we sell instead? You know I make a loss on the milkers; and beef cattle are fetching useless prices. Those cows I just brought in; three of them went straight to the byre and when I looked at them I realized we bred them; I sold them last back end; and I've just paid fifteen pounds less for each of them than I sold them for. Harry never killed them; they weren't worth selling at the price, he said, when I rang last night. So he kept them and sold them back to me. World's gone mad.'

Frankie thought of the conversation now. Buffet probably had farrowed. She heard Sam's heavy footsteps in the yard. He came in just as Spencer drove up at the gate and shouted for Shanie, who raced outside, dragging her schoolbag and her blazer, cannoned into her father, apologized and shot off. Spencer was late and she would be late and if she wasn't late she would get a star for attendance at the end of the term, and a paperback book as well. She loved reading, and she didn't want to spoil her record.

'Sorry,' she yelled, skidding round her father and dashing across the yard to the gate. Sam fielded the retriever pup and carried her indoors, as Peppy wanted to follow Shanie. Sam's face had lightened momentarily. But he set the pup on the floor, and sat at the table and picked up the morning paper, without saying a word. Cuckoo came in through the door, equally silent, and went to the sink to wash his hands.

'Breakfast, Cuckoo?' Frankie said, wondering why the man had come so early.

'Please, if it's no bother,' Cuckoo said. His mind was on something else and Frankie, serving fried luncheon meat, two eggs, and a mountain of fried potatoes, sighed. She was so sick of trouble. She made herself a slice of toast, poured the coffee, and took her cup and saucer to the fire. The old wicker chair creaked as she sat and Timbo jumped to her lap. He had become very much an indoor cat and Spencer had neutered him which made him pleasanter to live with. Sam liked a tomcat round the place, having a soft spot for kittens. The injured tail was healing but the stump was raw and furless.

'Now what's wrong?' Frankie asked at last, unable to stand the lowering silence. The men were carefully avoiding one another's eyes, which meant that something had happened that one of them was feeling righteous about, and knowing Sam, it was probably Cuckoo.

88

'I told him,' Cuckoo said. 'Wouldn't listen. Pig-headed as the old man was is Mr. Sam.'

Cuckoo had worked for Sam's father, and they had all grown old together. Very old, Frankie thought. She had read the paper before Sam came in and the news didn't make her feel any better. She must be starting a cold; or the middle-age megrims – and there was something to worry about. It was a thought that had never crossed her mind before. As if women didn't have enough to contend with!

'What has happened?' Frankie said. It sometimes took half a day to get any sense out of Cuckoo.

'Sow's farrowed,' Cuckoo said.

'It's been known to happen before,' Frankie said tartly.

'Fifteen bloody little monsters,' Cuckoo said.

'Fifteen what?' Frankie put her cup down so sharply that she spilled coffee into the saucer and over Timbo who spat and fled. He hated getting wet. He sat on the window sill indignantly washing his shoulder, and then curled up and glared, his tiger-striped stump tail lashing.

'They aren't all monsters,' Sam said, rustling the paper noisily, refusing to meet his sister's gaze.

'Eight of them look like monsters,' Cuckoo said. 'And God knows what the others are like inside. I told you what'd happen if we mated Buffet to her own father. It's not natural.'

'What sort of monsters?' Frankie asked, not wanting to hear the answer, but feeling she must know the worst; with visions of pigs with eight legs and two heads.

'Insides outside, and dead at birth,' Cuckoo said. 'The survivors look sickly too.'

Frankie set her mouth. No use saying I told you so. Sam always had to learn the hard way.

She walked outside, rather than use her tongue. Better not to aggravate him. It was bad enough. She went into the sty and looked down at Buffet who was stretched full length, very quiet, breathing oddly. A mass of blood lay on the sty floor.

Frankie ran.

'Haemorrhage,' she shouted, and both men were in the yard at once, pushing her aside, making for the sty. It looked too bad to expect anything but the worst. Frankie cleared the plates and fed the scraps to the cats and wished for the thousandth time that she had her horses. She missed the foal.

She was all grace, galloping in the wind, slim-legged, her mane tossing.

A motor bike sped by, somewhere along the main road, its engine revving. She shivered. The world was inimical, threatening, out of control.

She ached with longing for a man of her own and a home of her own; for children of her own and for quiet woods, and a horse to ride on, away from the farm. Shallow Dene was a weight on her shoulders, a burden on her back, and Shanie had tied her as surely as if she had been imprisoned.

She should have married Peter, all those years ago.

Unreasonable depression settled on her, so that she stared out over the gate and saw nothing, because her eyes were blurred with tears.

She was trapped by living and there was no escape.

Suddenly and infuriatingly a poem came into her mind.

> A weary lot is thine, fair maid,
>   A weary lot is thine.
> To pull the thorn thy brow to braid,
>   And press the rue for wine.

Sir Walter Scott had written it, so many years ago. How did it go on? Two lines were missing, but she knew the rest.

> No more of me, you knew,
>   My Love.
> No more of me you knew.

She lifted the pup and held it close against her and buried her head in Peppy's soft fur. The little bitch licked her face, and relaxed secure and blissfully happy.

Sam came out and stood beside her, unaware of any feeling but his own.

'Sow's dead,' he said. 'The last little beast was a real monster and it killed her. Enormous creature, more like a wild boar than a domestic pig, and with an outsize head. Thought they'd all come away. Should have fetched Spencer.'

'He wasn't there,' Frankie said. 'He took Shanie to school, remember. Surgery isn't till half past nine and anyway, it's too late now.'

'Running out of chicken feed. The lorry hasn't delivered,'

Sam said. 'Can you go over to Harry and see if he's got some to spare?'

Frankie reviewed her chores. The chickens and the little pigs to clean out; the animals to feed; the eggs to collect; the house to clean; there were no clean clothes for Shanie; and also the child needed her games kit next day – that wasn't washed either; and she had promised to give Sandy a hand with baking for the church fete. They were in charge of the cake stall, one that always sold out within an hour of starting; they never could have enough. She had said she'd bake bread and bread rolls and four sponge cakes; some pasties and some meringues. She hated day by day cooking but loved giving parties, or had loved them in the old days when there was time and money. Why on earth had she volunteered? She knew the days were always far too short.

'If Cuckoo can lend a hand with the cleaning and feeding, and you can make do with bread and cheese for lunch,' Frankie said, saying goodbye to all the spare time in her day. She could take the pup with her; she was very mischievous. If left in the house she chewed shoes and rugs; left in the yard she might escape and in any case, she had promised Shanie the dogs would never be left alone again. Even Sam was neurotic about his new collie. Pip slept in the house, which no sheepdog had ever done before; and the pup slept in Shanie's room. And that had stopped the nightmares.

Frankie's headachy feeling of foreboding increased as the morning went by. Cuckoo cleaned up the sty; there were seven baby pigs to be fed and no mother and that was going to be fun, Frankie thought irritably. She didn't want to touch the litter; the dead piglets had revolted her and though the survivors looked normal enough she had an irrational feeling that they might suddenly turn round and prove to be totally unpiglike. If Sam hadn't mated the sow like that she would be alive now and her loss was a greater blow than that of the litter, as she was a splendid brood sow. Her other two litters had been perfect, with fourteen piglets a time and no bother whatever.

But it wasn't fair to blame Sam all that much, she thought as she filled feeding bottles, and went out to see to the babies. Cuckoo was standing looking at them, a frown on his face.

'He should 'a listened,' the man said irritably, and marched outside, aware he shouldn't criticize the boss, but never able to hold his tongue on professional matters. Cuckoo was secretly convinced he was a much better farmer than Sam and could have made more of a go of the farm if he'd been lucky enough to be born there instead of in the tied cottage.

Frankie put the pup down on the floor in front of the passenger seat of her mini and drove off, gears crashing. She was an erratic driver as far as the engine was concerned, though ultra careful. She turned into the lane.

A moment later there was an appalling crash of metal.

Sam and Cuckoo ran.

Tich had turned into the lane, sent by Ken to see if the horses were about. He was riding his bike at speed, cornering fast, forgetting that cars drove down from the farm. They came so rarely that he was used to an empty road.

He hit Frankie's mini on the passenger side, catapulting Peppy across the car into her legs. Peppy, terrified, bit her mistress's ankle.

Frankie was held firmly by her seat belt. It snatched at her and she was bruised and sick and sore. Tich lay on the ground, blood pouring from a cut on his head. Sandy, who had heard the noise, raced back when she saw the two men were already coping and was dialling 999, her voice urgent.

Sam knelt over Tich.

'Pretty badly hurt,' he said. 'Better not move him.'

He put his coat over the man. Sandy came back with a blanket from her bed to put over Tich, and looked at the wrecked motor bike.

'I never did like those things,' she said. 'Are you O.K., love?'

Frankie nodded.

The car was a mess, the wing buckled, the door dented, and the centre pillar had moved, which meant no car for weeks and she needed the car for shopping, and for ferrying Shanie around. It was another disaster. Her mind went back to her horoscope. A bad day for travelling. You could say that again.

It was a day that turned into a nightmare, with the police questioning her; with a statement to be made, with an injection as the result of Peppy's bite; the pup was bruised and miserable and Spencer gave her an injection too; there were the pigs to bottle-feed; and she was now without feed for the chickens and she hadn't done the shopping or Shanie's washing, and one rib felt as if it was cracked and she couldn't stop shivering.

'Never rains but it pours,' Cuckoo said, sitting like an improbable and grotesque Madonna holding a little pig upside down and fighting it to make it take the bottle.

'Reckon this one's got no gullet,' Cuckoo said morosely, and Frankie, looking at the little pig she held, felt an overwhelming revulsion.

The post, coming a few minutes later, distracted her from thoughts that were becoming increasingly unpleasant. She returned the piglet to the straw and slit open the envelope before realizing it was addressed to Sam.

Not that it mattered.

Sam would have told her. She found herself staring at an incredible demand for £57,000 income tax, and sickness engulfed her, so that she had to clutch at the table. It was insane. They hadn't that much money even if they sold all the farm and all the stock.

She stood there with the demand note in her hands and the tears she had been fighting all day pouring down her cheeks.

Cuckoo set the piglet down in the cat basket, where it snuffled and went to sleep, and patted Frankie awkwardly on the shoulder.

'There, there,' he said idiotically, as if she were a child.

Blindly she handed him the demand note.

He stared at it, bewildered.

'Dear Heaven,' he said. 'What has Mr. Sam been doing?'

CHAPTER THIRTEEN

SAM stared at the demand note as if the world had turned upside down and shaken him off into space. He couldn't believe it. It didn't make sense. None of it made sense. He had paid his tax. It was insane. He rang the bank, who were baffled, wondering if he had missed out on surtax in past years when the farm was rich. You could be assessed ten years late; or had he failed on the death duties? He slammed down the receiver, and turned to face Frankie, who was still feeling shocked and sick. Her leg hurt and her ribs hurt. She wanted to go to bed and she was sitting there like a monument to Motherhood holding a squalling little pig that didn't know how to suck.

She felt exactly like a character from *Alice in Wonderland*. The baby that turnéd into a pig. Well, this one wouldn't turn into a baby. She stared down at it, at its small eyes and pink snout and wondered why on earth she was bothering.

Shanie erupted into the room.

'Where's Peppy? Can I feed the pig? Frankie, are you all right?'

'No, I'm not all right,' Frankie said irritably. 'Some man on a motor bike crashed into my car; and my ribs hurt and Peppy bit me and the pig won't feed.'

'A man on a motor bike?' Shanie said. There had been motor bikes in the lane the afternoon all the animals were hurt. Sam saw her expression. He lifted the receiver and rang the police. Easy enough to check the bike for fingerprints. The man had a fractured skull and was very ill indeed. If it was one of the vandals, Sam found he didn't even care.

Shanie took the piglet, and the bottle, and enlarged the hole in the teat. She was always good with baby animals. No point in telling her about the deformed piglets, but she had to know the sow was dead. Frankie sat drinking the tea that Cuckoo had made, wondering when to tell the child.

'I suppose this is Buffet's. Did she die?' Shanie asked.

'Aye, one of her monsters killed her. Bled to death.' Cuckoo didn't turn to look at Frankie. He knew she would disapprove.

'What monsters?' Shanie asked.

'Cuckoo!' Frankie said.

'Shanie's going to inherit this farm. Right?' Cuckoo said. 'And what use is a farmer who doesn't know about farming? Your Dad mated Buffet to Thomas Clockett. Her own father. And it didn't work. Too close and half the litter were deformed.' Cuckoo faced Frankie defiantly.

'Dad said they might be; he knew he was taking a risk,' Shanie said. She mopped the little pig's face, and took it outside, without further comment.

'That kid beats me,' Frankie said. 'Two months ago there

94

would have been such a carry on. She doesn't even seem to care.'

'She's growing up,' Cuckoo said. 'And going to be a rare beauty. You and Mr. Sam'll have your work cut out to keep the bees away from the honey pot.'

How do you armour them against the world, Frankie wondered as Shanie came back into the room. Sam had gone into the little office in the dairy to try and telephone his accountant. But he was a one-man business and was working on a major account in South Africa until the end of the month.

'Phone the Inland Revenue,' Frankie suggested.

'And find out I've got only two weeks to pay,' Sam said. 'I'm going to the Roost tonight. Get drunk as a lord; what the hell's the use of staying sober?'

He turned to the door, to find Shanie staring at him, holding Timbo in her arms.

'I don't mean it, love,' he said, rightly interpreting the expression on her face. 'Just a saying, that's all.'

She set the cat down gently. Nothing felt safe any more. Suppose Frankie had been killed that morning in the car crash?

Nothing was safe. Her mother had died. She couldn't even remember her mother. But Frankie had been there, all the time, to run to for comfort, to laugh with, to play with. Sometimes in the long winter evenings Frankie knitted and Shanie read aloud and the animals listened. There had been security in the farmhouse, sanctuary when the doors were shut and the lights were on, and the place shut up for the night.

Now she listened for footsteps in the lane, listened for the sudden cry of a dog or a cat in pain; for the bellowing of a frightened calf. She and Sandy crept like thieves to Tranter's to tame the cub and the kitten. They were so very wild. They hid still at footsteps, though they ate the food that was brought for them. They were trapped in the cellar until they were big enough to jump. Would the cub ever jump, Shanie sometimes wondered, and then was in trouble at school for daydreaming.

And at night the pipes sounded, at dusk, till dark, and sometimes behind them came the tramp of feet. She never dared look out of the window. After the pipes came the screech of a hunting owl, and she knew that at Tranter's there were uncanny sounds; squeaks and squeals and solid thumps; crashes as the cub and the kitten ran through the cellars, chasing one another, delighting in movement.

Sandy went daily with food for them. They had named the kitten Tomas, and the cub Tuska. She could see the small heads, watching her intently from a safe distance, but neither moved to eat until she had gone. Shanie joined her in the evening. Both Sam and Frankie hated the child being alone in the lane now. Shanie chafed at the restriction. She had never had to take care before. The fields and the woods had been her refuge, and she missed the long walks during the weekend, when she had spent hours bird and animal watching. She hadn't even seen the young squirrels this summer.

Sam was impressed with his daughter, who, since Frankie had been out of action, had been helping around the farm far more than usual. She was up without telling at dawn to help him bring the cows in and fix the milking cups; she knew how to work the machine, and even how to kick when it proved temperamental, as it was second-hand when he bought it and was now showing its age.

She had learned from Cuckoo how to stand softly beside a cow reluctant to let down its milk, and soothe it in a hissing hum, so that it rubbed against her hand and relaxed. She was as quick as he to wash down hindquarters and udders before milking; and fastidious about her hands, and amused Cuckoo by supervising the scalding of the churns, telling him all she had recently learned in a school hygiene lesson about infection.

'What'll they teach you next?' Cuckoo asked.

'They taught us sex, but it's silly,' Shanie said.

'Silly?' Cuckoo looked at her, a little startled, wondering what on earth the lesson had been about.

'They don't know anything about it,' Shanie said. 'They didn't even know you have to put a small bull on a first-time cow if she hasn't calved, or the calf will be too big. And they didn't know about the boar trolley to keep the boar from crushing the sow. It was only about people and that's not a bit interesting!'

Cuckoo managed to stifle a snort, and wondered what Shanie's teacher would make of the conversation.

'Who told you about it then?' he asked.

'Miss Hunt. She's only just come from college, and she

doesn't even know the difference between a short-horn and a Friesian; she thought all cows were black and white!'

'Town people don't know they're born, let alone know about animals, poor things,' Cuckoo said, with a world of pity in his voice. It was hard to understand how anyone grew up sane in a place so deprived that the only flowers that grew were set in rows in the parks and the only animals were a few pet dogs and perhaps a police horse.

'Hannibal's got a sore leg,' Shanie said. 'He keeps on licking it.'

'You shouldn't be around that bull,' Cuckoo told her. 'He's a wild one. Better tell your Dad about the leg.'

'Dad's waiting for Mr. Tomson to come home from South Africa. He's fretting himself silly about that old tax,' Shanie said, not knowing how much the demand was for, and puzzled by the fact that both Sam and Frankie were so short-tempered that life was impossible. Frankie's rib must hurt; but Sam was beyond all reason and that wasn't like her father. He hadn't drunk too much in the Roost, but one night he might and come home and beat them all up, or attack the animals.

The week crawled past.

Sam wished he knew how to get in touch with his accountant. The huge sum of money haunted him; the figures danced at him in bed at night, and he couldn't eat for worrying. He didn't know how he could raise it; they already had a huge overdraft at the bank. Suppose the bank called it in? Could they dispossess him, sell up everything he had and what the hell would they all do then? He would have to take a job as a farmhand on another man's farm; he wasn't fit for anything else. Frankie could probably go back to her old partner and breed horses again. But what of the child? Four years before she could leave school. Indigestion settled like a nagging knife under Sam's ribs, and his temper worsened daily.

The kitten and the cub were ten weeks old when Sam went down to the Roost one night, and found Ken sitting in the corner, his sharp eyes watching as always. Ken was puzzled by the absence of the horses, and he missed Tich who was going to be out of action for a very long time. Also the police had discovered that Tich had been one of the men at the farm on that Saturday afternoon. He had left fingerprints in the kitchen that matched those on his bike. Ken wanted to know what else had been discovered. He had worn gloves and was sure no one had seen them.

Jim Taylor watched the man, feeling, as usual, uneasy at his presence.

Sam ordered drinks for himself and Cuckoo. He liked bitter and Cuckoo preferred mild. He took them over to the table nearest the blazing fire.

'Shanie's getting a good eye for an animal,' Sam said. 'I took her to look at a horse the other day.'

Ken drank his beer fast and went to the bar for a refill. He moved to a table that was closer to the men, and eavesdropped unashamedly.

He wanted that mare and the foal. Business was bad; never had been so bad, and there was a man down south who would give a good price for her. And he was losing the lads. Smithy was useless, so demoralized by the killing that he had reverted to almost total stupidity and was quite unsafe for work. One thing – Smithy wouldn't talk. He was too afraid, and Ken had ways of making him even more afraid.

He missed Tich. Tich was a daredevil, ready for anything. The lad had brains too which was more than the other two had. They would follow where Tich led; but Ken didn't want to be involved closely with them. He liked Tich to give the orders. That afternoon at the farm had been a mistake.

Cuckoo had taken his time answering Sam's statement.

'She's a farmer's daughter, all right,' Cuckoo said. 'She's got your old man's touch. You ought to see her in the field with that bull. He's as gentle as an unhatched chick with her. She was bathing that leg for him yesterday when I went to do it, saying it looked sore and she thought he'd like some soothing lotion on it. He just stood there and let her and he scares me stiff when I do it. Always afraid he'll turn on me like that old devil over at Layton's before the war.'

'There was a nasty brute at Tranter's in old Ben's day,' Sam said. 'Pinned his stockman to the wall. That was the beginning of Tranter's bad luck. Old Ben never got over that accident. The man was killed and his wife committed suicide. Ben started to go funny after that.'

Sam had been a young man then, enjoying his life of freedom after the years of the war, which he had just missed, and regretted. He would have liked to be a Battle of Britain pilot. Instead he had been a schoolboy and the war had ended before he got a chance to show anyone what he was made of. Then the old man had gone downhill and the farm had settled round his neck like a dirty great millstone going backwards through the years, unable to keep up with modern needs. He ought to have new barns and new stalls for the cattle and a new parlour for the milking and new machinery. No time for hammer and nails to mend anything. No time for living. Only work.

He swallowed his pint and ordered another.

'Talking of Tranter's,' Spencer Dayson said, coming over from the bar where he had been talking to Jim about his brood mare, 'have you heard what they're doing to it?'

'To Tranter's?' Cuckoo asked.

'Aye.' Spencer spread himself over the chair and pulled out his pipe, tamping the tobacco down, and lighting it before he spoke again. Jackson and Johnson were with him and came to sit beside him, their muscular brown and black curly-haired bodies hard against his leg, their long ears dangling. Cuckoo patted each warm flank. He missed having a dog. A cat wasn't really the same. Couldn't bring it boozing with you for one thing. He grinned into his beer at the vision this provoked.

'The council are going to knock it down.'

'Knock down Tranter's? They'll have old Ben after them. He won't lie still,' Cuckoo said.

'It's been condemned as unsafe,' Spencer said. 'It's twenty years since Ben went. It's evidently on top of some caves that are thought to be old mine workings and has been settling. They're going to raze it, and to add that bit of ground to the park. It sticks out like a sore stye anyway, projecting into the place. It was the old home farm for the Manse, of course, which is why it's built there.'

'Place won't be the same without Tranter's,' Cuckoo grumbled. 'Don't see why they can't let well alone. It don't do to interfere with haunted buildings. All hell'll be let loose if they knock that down.'

'When are they starting?' Sam asked.

'Very soon. It's been approved for ages it seems. It was just a matter of when. The place has belonged to the council all these years, along with the Manor and the park. They took it over when Ben died. His nephew sold it for a song, but no one's ever done a thing about it; it was pretty far gone twenty years ago.'

99

'It's not doing much good there,' Sam said. 'No one could afford to rebuild the place now.'

'Nobody'd want to,' Cuckoo said. 'Not with yells and screams and rustles. There's enough funny noises by day. I wouldn't want to be there at night.'

'Old houses always are noisy,' Spencer said. 'The wind in the empty rooms, whistling and whining. Probably jays nest there, and birds can make some ear-splitting noises. Like that cock pheasant behind me at daybreak, and then Sam's guinea fowl start up. It would only need one of them to run off and meet in Tranter's and you'd have enough noises to frighten most townsfolk.'

Cuckoo laughed his wheezy groaning chuckle.

'Like the night that young couple came to my cottage,' he said. 'They thought there was a drunk or someone having a heart attack in the ditch. Very funny noises, they said. Heavy breathing and rumbling sounds. I went along with them to find out. Dark as the inside of a bay mare and raining too.'

He laughed again, his small face creasing into a network of lines, as he struggled to control himself.

'What was it?' Spencer asked.

'Sam's cows. Lying against the hedge, all breathing together and rumbling away as they brought up their cud. Must say if you don't know, a herd breathing together at night sounds proper creepy. You couldn't see them, either. Dark against the hedge, and no moon. The young couple were shook up, though. They didn't know what to say. They'd been scared silly by what they thought was a very sick man and it was only a load of cattle.'

'I frightened myself once,' Spencer said. 'I went into my boss's kitchen the first day of my first job. I didn't know he brought animals under anaesthesia there to keep warm and out of the way till they came round. My tea was laid on the table. I had the whole place to myself, no one in at all, and then this noise began. I'd never before sat with a recovering animal; always treated them, and then went. This noise came from behind an armchair near the fire and it was some time before I summoned enough courage to go and see what was there. I had visions of an intruder, hiding, breathing heavily, and ready to pounce out on me.'

'What was it?' Sam asked.

'A cat recovering from being spayed. Heavy breathing

wasn't in it. I thought something must have gone wrong and rang my boss up. He was at a dinner party.'

'What did he say?' asked Cuckoo.

'He listened and said nothing was wrong. And then he went back to eat and got worried and came home. By then the cat was nearly recovered and nothing was wrong. He was rather rude,' Spencer added. 'But we all have to learn. Sometimes if I'm alone in the house Jackson and Johnson make the most extraordinary noises. And they hear ghosts and bark at shadows.'

'There's nothing like a dog for company,' Cuckoo said wistfully.

'I knew there was something,' Spencer said. 'I've got a problem. A Border collie, eight years old. She belonged to an elderly lady who's died. She'd be perfect for you, Cuckoo. I don't want to put her down. She's a nice animal and several more years in her yet. She'll work for anyone. I had her on the lawn this afternoon. She's still fretting, though it's been seven weeks since her mistress died. Someone at the local dog club has been looking after her, but she's a bitch of her own who won't tolerate the newcomer and went for her. I had to put seven stitches in her leg and promised to do something about her.'

Cuckoo sat very still.

Only that day he'd been wishing extra hard. Eight years old. She'd be steady and sober and a head on his feet at night, and an animal to take about again. Be trouble with the cat but they'd soon sort that.

'When can I have her?' he asked. 'Next one's on me, to celebrate. I've been too long without a dog.'

'It's me birthday tomorrow,' he added suddenly and unexpectedly. 'Thirty-two.' He winked at Spencer.

'Then it's drinks on the house and here's to the new dog,' Jim said, bringing over spilling pints, the creamy head foaming down the tankard sides.

A dog again. He hadn't wanted to start another pup when old Tiber died. Too tiring, without a woman in the house to help with training and all those meals. It would be good to have a dog to talk to.

He walked home whistling under his breath.

Ken stayed till closing time. He stood outside the Roost, listening as Jim locked up. Bolts were shut and doors were barred, and the pub's two guard dogs were fierce. No use trying to get at the till, though there must be a tidy sum there night after night.

Softly down the lane, came the whisper of bagpipes, rising and falling, a cadence on the wind. Ken shivered; daft to think of haunting, but the lads were saying there were ghosts in the lane and there were noises at Tranter's all right, though if the old place was settling, then that would account for it.

The pipes were coming towards him, but there was nothing to be seen. He pulled his coat collar up round his head, against the wind and the rain and wished he had a torch. The lane was very dark and rutted. He plunged his foot in a puddle, soaking his sock to the ankle, and swore.

Tranter's was black against the sky. Looming eerily, one chimney leaning over at a crazy angle. The pipes were closer. And then, loud and clear, came an appalling eldritch scream, followed by the crash of iron against stone.

Ken ran.

The pipes keened triumphantly behind him, and inside Tranter's the cub lifted a dazed head, having jumped at the kitten and missed his footing, so that he fell and bruised a leg, squealing in pain as he landed.

CHAPTER FOURTEEN

THE days passed swiftly. Sam, obsessed by his enormous tax demand, was surly, worry upsetting his digestion, preventing him from sleeping. He wished he used a big firm of accountants instead of one man. John Tomson rarely took on small accounts; Sam was a longstanding acquaintance, and had been in need of help. But the arrangement had its inconveniences.

Frankie had to rest her arm; lifting and carrying hurt her sore ribs. Sandy came willingly to help on the farm and Cuckoo put in more hours than seemed possible every day. Susabell had a new calf; and the remaining piglets grew. Shanie, bottle-feeding them, found herself very lonely; wishing she had friends who could come to the farm; wishing she could return alone to the woods; wishing her father would stop snapping at them; wishing that she could take the kitten and the cub, and walk both animals on a lead. She pictured herself, featured on television, as the girl who tamed a fox cub. Daydreams substituted for friends. No one she knew was interested in the farm.

Sometimes she walked out to talk to Hannibal, who was besotted about the child, listening for her footsteps, rubbing his head against her arm, accepting cattle cake from her fingers, quieted when she spoke to him. He was a restless uneasy animal, stamping in the stable at night, tossing the straw. Sam padlocked the door. He was taking no chances.

He hated the mornings most, getting up early, walking into a silent world, where there were hiding places in the barns and anyone might lurk. He was convinced the vandalism was either the work of a lunatic, in which case it was unpredictable; or was a planned attack by someone out to steal the horses. These days, men would take anything that they could convert into cash. Peter Warwick, at Piper's Passion, had lost fifty sheep two nights running, rustled expertly by men with trained collies, observed by a passer-by who, seeing the dogs, thought the sheep were being collected legally, even if the time was rather odd. Men often worked overtime, to fit more jobs into an overshort day.

It was ridiculous for a grown man to be afraid, but fear had become part of him; fear for his stock; for his livelihood; and for Shanie. The child had recovered much of her confidence. They had been untroubled for some time, and she was forgetting. Sam did not want the memory to fade; and he did not want to keep it alive. But he was afraid for his daughter. She was young, and vulnerable, and men who could break a kitten's neck would not hesitate to hurt a child who got in their way.

Shanie wanted, more than anything in the world, to tame the cub and the kitten; to arrive with them following at her heels and show them, nonchalantly, to Spencer and Sandy and Cuckoo. Tranter's was not so far away. If she crept there, very quietly, instead of going to Sandy's, no one would be any the wiser. She need only stay for half an hour, and then she could race to Sandy, pretending she had just left home. Seven for a secret. It would be wonderful to have a secret, all her own. And if she crept through the long grass, and watched for strangers, she was sure to be safe. No use asking permission.

Neither Frankie nor Sam would give it, and even Cuckoo and Sandy told her to take care, and watched for her coming and going if they were around.

Within a week of her decision the cub and the kitten fed from the bowl at her feet. By the end of two weeks, they allowed her to touch them, and excitement grew. No one noticed that she did not go directly to Sandy from school, but slipped through the elf field, and across the cowfield, using the high hedges for cover, and then slipping swiftly over the lane, through the hedge into the field to approach Tranter's from the rear, and be greeted at last by a soft purr from the kitten and a strange little hissing whimper from the cub as they nosed her pocket.

Sandy often wondered at the child's elation, as she sped up the path, cheeks flushed and eyes alight, but she put it down to release from tension, and to the new kittens born to Tanetta only a week ago. Tan never minded sharing. She showed off her litter to all comers, purring proudly, and when she was tired of baby minding, absent-mindedly dumped them on Sandy's bed, and stalked around the cottage declaring she was famished and how about food, fast.

'She can almost talk,' Shanie said on one of these occasions. She had not visited the two little animals that afternoon. She hoped to cadge some food from Sandy, as Frankie had been complaining that the dogs were stealing food at home and was beginning to notice that there were discrepancies in the pantry.

Sandy had been baking. Shanie went off with scones and cakes for her tea, and some dried cat food she had begged for Timbo. Sandy had no suspicions as the child ran off down the lane. There was no one about, and it was such a short way to the farm. She tidied up the living room and returned the kittens to the box behind the big armchair, where Tanetta rediscovered them with loud purrs and swift licks, greeting them as if she had been away for a year instead of a bare fifteen minutes. Sandy could set the clock by the cat. At six that evening she would once more take the kittens and put them on the bed, apparently preferring them there while she was feeding.

Sandy's rich voice rang out in the lane and Cuckoo, returning briefly to his own home for his tea, grinned to himself. He enjoyed listening. He loved music of all kinds, and his hi-fi equipment and collection of records was his main hobby.

He hummed the tune that Sandy was singing and watched Shanie duck into the elf field. She was safe enough there. He went into the kitchen to prepare food for his new bitch.

Shanie heard the singing and smiled to herself. Sandy's bellows could be heard up and down the lane. Sandy was always in top voice when she coasted down the hill on her bicycle singing hymns.

> Mine eyes have seen the glory
> Of the coming of the Lord.

The stirring words followed Shanie all the way to Tranter's. She paused for a moment near the farm, wondering whether to go and get Peppy. The pup was far too boisterous for the cub and the kitten. So she had to be left at home. Anyway, Frankie would have fed the dogs and it wasn't fair to take them out when they wanted to sleep. She could play with Peppy later.

The hedge branches, dripping after rain, soaked her anorak as she slipped through the field, taking care to approach unseen. She crept between the hedge and the shrubs that bordered it, overgrown from long years of neglect, uncut, shutting out the light. It was creepy in the garden, crawling under the bramble tunnels to reach the cellar opening and lower herself inside.

Tomas came swiftly to greet her, rubbing extravagantly round her legs. Tuska was more cautious, but he too came to sniff at the food and eat it from her hand. Shanie knelt beside them, totally absorbed. There were creaks and groans from the ageing wood, and a soft sound as if earth were spilling, but she was too absorbed to notice.

She had begun to explore the cellars and found an old cat basket, in remarkably good repair. It was necessary to introduce animals very slowly to new things. She lined it with paper and put the food inside. Both cub and kitten jumped in fearlessly. They had fed in the basket before and it held no terrors. Cuckoo had taught Shanie well. As far as animals went it was always softly, softly, catchee monkey.

Both animals were feeding.

Gently, cautiously, Shanie closed the lid, and slipped the

catch. She would teach them to accept the basket and then she would carry them home. The vandals hadn't been back. No one had been near the farm. She knew nothing of Ken's visit, or of her father's fear. Neither he nor Frankie wanted to alarm the child too much.

She ought to go.

There was a rustling from the basket, and an irritated snarl. She bent to open the catch.

There was a sudden crack, a thud, and a roar of sound. There had been rain all summer, more rain than anyone could remember, and the sodden earth beneath Tranter's had slipped away. There was nothing but darkness and terrifying noise. Crash and thump and slipping walls, a roar of collapsing timber as the blind windows vanished and the roof fell in and nothing was left but a vast pile of rubble where the dust settled slowly and the bricks shifted and slid.

Then came silence.

Tranter's lay dead under the sky, and no one was near.

CHAPTER FIFTEEN

SAM heard the thunderous noise. He raced down the lane to look. Tranter's had vanished; there was dust over the rubble, and nothing remained of the house. He walked back to Sandy's to find that Shanie had already left. She must have returned to the farm while he had been investigating.

But there was no sign of the child. Cuckoo searched the elf field, calling. Hannibal lowed uneasily. He was out in the field and needed to be brought in for the night. Cuckoo went to fetch the bull, while Sam and Frankie searched the barns, wondering if perhaps one of the cats had had kittens there, and the child was crouched, absorbed, as always, by the spectacle of new motherhood.

Trouble, the tame boar that Frankie had hand-reared two years before, grunted irritably as they passed his sty. He had become too much of a nuisance to be allowed to roam free. He hated confinement. It had been much more fun when he could invade the kitchen and the cow byres and charge at Hannibal and see the bull lower his massive head.

Frankie went on searching and calling while Sam finished cleaning up the milking parlour. Cuckoo had taken his bitch and was scouring the fields, fear nudging uneasily. Suppose the vandals had come back? Suppose they had harmed the child? Cuckoo began to hunt through the grass, to search along the ditch, to pull aside bushes, looking for the materialization of his anxiety.

A child is missing.

She hadn't been gone for long, Frankie thought, calling again, looking up and down the lane, starting at the sounds of footsteps, but it was only Sandy, who had heard Cuckoo shout and come running.

'She must be somewhere around,' Sandy said. 'It's not like Shanie to run off alone; not these days when she knows we all worry.'

Sam whistled his sheepdog. Pip came trotting, eager for an unexpected walk. Frankie brewed tea, and telephoned the police. Sandy took her cudgel and walked down the lane, and then realized that the noise she had heard earlier on was Tranter's. She stared at the rubble, appalled. The cub and the kitten were somewhere beneath it. And suppose . . .

Terror caught at her throat and she ran back to the farmhouse.

'Suppose Shanie went back to Tranter's? To see the cub and the kitten . . .'

The kitchen clock ticked on, an insistent irritating sound hurrying the minutes that added up too fast. Hannibal lowed in his stall. It was dark. It was cold. Frankie shivered. She had not realized how time had fled past. Why hadn't she thought of Tranter's? Sam had told her what had happened. Fear for the child had driven all thought of the kitten and the cub out of her head. If Shanie had gone there . . . would she go alone when she knew that everyone was afraid for her safety?

But children had short memories.

Frankie had a banging headache and a sickness that wouldn't go. Sam came in from the fields; rain was falling and his coat was wet. He stared at the two women. Sandy began to explain about the kitten and the cub. One of the policemen had come back and was listening.

'She might have gone there,' Sam said heavily. He knew his daughter too well. Small animals were irresistible.

'She's been messing about with the old whelping kennel,' Cuckoo said suddenly. 'Repairing the wire, and strengthening the door fastening. It would make a good cage for a kitten and a cub. Suppose . . .'

But he couldn't suppose. He could only see the tumbled bricks and remember the noises. So that was what had caused it. He had a brief disastrous vision of the child lying under the rubble, and struck the table with his hand so hard that the crockery bounced and the dogs fled into the corner.

'We didn't take enough care,' Sam said desolately.

'You can't watch them every second of the day,' the policeman said. His own small son was an imp, who needed surveillance from morning till night and exhausted his mother.

'We'll get a gang to search the rubble; but don't give up searching everywhere else. She might be in the fields. She might have slipped and fallen; it's rough ground all round here.'

She might be in the elf field, Cuckoo thought and fetched his torch to search again, unable to sit still. Sam went out into the yard and once more searched the barns. He couldn't stand the sight of Frankie's face, drawn and aged so suddenly, her eyes shadowed and enormous. Sandy, a dumpy anxious figure, was standing, forlorn, in her ragged gardening macintosh held together by a piece of string, as she couldn't find her belt. Her hair needed a comb, but she had no time to think of herself. She could not get rid of the vision of Tranter's lying under the sky, with the cub and the kitten beneath it, and the growing certainty that Shanie had been up to something there; unable to resist the unlikely pair, planning to tame them and bring them home, feeling more secure as the weeks went by and nothing unpleasant happened.

Cuckoo found nothing in the field. He walked up to the Robbers' Roost, and returned with all the men behind him. Grim-faced men with anxious eyes who could not sit and drink quietly when they knew a child was missing. The landlord was with them. And so was Ken. Sam looked at the man uneasily, wishing he had not come. Behind, at the inn, Sue cleared up the glasses, her thoughts milling, wishing she could go with the search party, but she could not leave the boys alone. She felt insecure with Jim gone, and on an impulse went out to shut the animals away and then to bar her own front door and bring both the Alsatian guard dogs inside. The exodus of men had disturbed her horribly. Eyes glanced into eyes, not voicing thoughts that embraced all sorts of unpleasant possibilities.

Sam found he could not talk to the men who had come to help, and who were planning the field of search. All very well for them. It wasn't their child who was involved. There was a constriction in his throat and a prickle behind his eyes. Dear God, if only the child were unharmed. If anyone had touched her . . . he would kill any man responsible as sure as day dawned each morning. Dear God, where could they look? Was she really under Tranter's? He took the big torch and began a useless search of the farm buildings again, hunting through barn and byre and stable with the dog close at his heels, watching every movement and occasionally obligingly sniffing around, although Pip had no idea what they were hunting. She was no use for tracking.

'She'll be O.K. Always falls on her feet, does our Shanie,' Cuckoo said, not meaning it, but needing to do something to ease Sam's desperate expression. His legs were aching. He had the screws something cruel; all this wet weather, pouring down day after day. He couldn't remember a summer like it. Grey skies and dismal trees and the stream full and riverlike and still rising, and there was another worry flaring to life. Suppose she had gone down to look for the grebe on the pool? He'd told her about them the day before. Never had grebe in the park till then and the child loved birds, as well as all other animals.

The men had gone, spread out in the fields and the flash of torches gleamed and was gone as they walked among trees, and were hidden by the tall trunks. Ken had gone with them, but his quick eyes had noted the stable and the heavy padlock. So the mare was still there. It was a thought to ponder. One day, soon, he'd get her and the foal would follow where his mother went. A piece of cake and better without the lads. It wouldn't take long to go home and come back again with the horse box. He could do as he had intended before and lead the mare across the field to the gate and the lay-by. It was a useful lay-by, a piece of the old road, sheltered by high hedges and quite invisible unless you were actually parked on the half moon of road. The box could stay there for several days, and no one would think twice about it.

A second police car drew up in the yard. The two policemen came into the kitchen, ducking to avoid the rafter that was the cause of Sam's stoop. Both were worried now. It was time to consider the child's disappearance as more than a casual incident. She had no friends near to visit. No one had set eyes on her since Cuckoo saw her ducking through the elf field, trying to remain unseen. She wouldn't have run away; they had checked with her school. She had had a very good day, and was not the kind of child to get into trouble.

'There will be a gang along to search the rubble,' the bigger policeman said. He was a massive man, well over six feet, his uniform tight on a muscular body. 'And the dogs will be out soon. Is there anywhere she could have fallen? A quarry? Or a little cliff?'

'We've looked,' Sam said. It had been the first thing he did; down in the tiny hollow where they had had a bomb drop during the war, now overgrown with bramble; and at the foot of the little cliff where the foal had fallen. The swollen stream could have carried her away. Where the hell did you start to look?

Spencer, walking into the yard with Jackson and Johnson at his heels, was grim-faced. He had known about the cub and the kitten, and was sure the child would have gone to Tranter's on some ploy of her own concerning them; she had been recovering from fear; and Tranter's wasn't far away; it was within sight of the farm, or had been until the cave-in. If she were under that lot, there was not the slightest hope. The ground had fallen away and the weight of masonry alone would have killed her.

He had searched through the woods with the dogs; had left his evening meal uneaten and left his wife to attend to his resident patients. He lit a cigarette from the stub of one that was only half-smoked, sucked at it several times and then stubbed it savagely in the saucer of a tea-cup that one of the policemen was drinking from. Frankie, irritated, pushed across an ashtray but said nothing. She had become mentally numb. She wanted to go to Tranter's and tear the bricks away with her bare hands; wished they had never found the cub and the kitten; and if it hadn't been for the vandals, none of this would have happened. It all stemmed from that one day, back in time, twisting their lives out of the ordinary path into a nightmare.

Sam came indoors and went out again, to test the padlock on the bull's stall; he didn't want Hannibal out to add to the confusion. He had penned the ganders, and Frankie had put the pup in her bedroom and closed the door, lest Peppy vanished too. She could never face Shanie if the pup were lost.

Beyond the trees the church clock struck eleven. Jackson and Johnson settled themselves on the rug in front of the Aga, rejoicing in forbidden warmth. Cuckoo was humming, an irritating monotonous sound that went on endlessly. Only the dogs were unaffected by the atmosphere in the room. The two policemen, waiting now for the dog vans, had no comfort to offer.

Frankie could not bear to stay with the men. She went out into the yard. Light from the kitchen window flung across the cobbles. The wind teased a straw. There was a chill in the air. An owl hooted, long and low, a forlorn requiem, and the rain began again, a steady drenching downpour.

A car passed up the lane and then a lorry, making for Tranter's. Spencer and Sam walked out into the yard, neither man speaking. Pip followed and Sam took her indoors and shut her away with the pup. The two pointers followed Spencer, placidly at heel. He opened his car door and they jumped inside and settled on the rug on the floor of the big estate vehicle. Nose on paw, they sighed deeply, and curled to sleep.

Cuckoo tagged behind them.

A cow bellowed in the field. The sky had blacked out the moon. The men were wet through, hair lying damply on cold faces, soaking trouser legs flapping, hands chilled to the bone. Hastily-rigged searchlights, running off a small generator that throbbed mercilessly flooded the desolation that was Tranter's. Sam shuddered and joined the ring of men who stood within the light and stared.

One of the policemen spoke and echoed the words for all of them.

'Dear God. Where do we begin?'

CHAPTER SIXTEEN

SANDY joined them some minutes later. She had revisited the house, checked on the cats and locked them away. She walked up the darkened lane, afraid of the emptiness beyond the hedgerows. The night had been loud with unusual noise, and she jumped at every sound. She was cursing herself bitterly for not insisting that the kitten and the cub were trapped and brought home. It had been insane to hide them; the vandals wouldn't come back. No one had come back. One stupid isolated incident and they had all acted absurdly.

'If only we'd known about the beasties,' Cuckoo said.

'If wishes were horses then beggars would ride,' Sandy snapped. It was bad enough for her to blame herself, but it was fifty times worse when other people did so. Cuckoo, who had only been filling the endless minutes with empty words, was hurt and said no more.

The lane was bright with light and loud with noise. Sam had brought his Land-Rover and there was a police Land-Rover, both parked with headlights streaming over the rubble. A crane on a lorry towered inimically above them, an improbable monster, waiting to drag away beams and girders. Sandy stared at the house, hating it. It had always been an unlucky house. Some places were doomed to give trouble. Others, like hers, were happy and welcoming and so was Shallow Dene.

Men were working now; every spare policeman, and some who should have been off-duty; men from the Robbers', who had not stayed to drink, but came to help; men from the building site on the other side of the town, hastily collected by police, needing professional assistance. Lorries and cars were parked against the hedges; bicycles and motor bikes; and three dog vans, spilling men and gay tail-wagging Alsatians, delighted to be working, and quite untouched by the general air of gloom.

Frankie took the men back to the farmhouse, and watched as the dogs set off on the child's trail. She could not stay alone. She returned to Tranter's and began to help lift the bricks, one by one, passing them to Sandy who stacked them on the ground behind her for Cuckoo to take away.

Similar small chains were working all around the house, desperately anxious not to cause anything to shift.

There was a sharp bark. Frankie turned her head. The first police dog was pelting along towards her, nose down, hot on a scent. He circled the rubble and barked again, lifting his head, looking at his master, and began to paw at the rubble.

'She's there,' the policeman said.

The second dog joined them.

And then the third.

There was no possible doubt, and there was no consolation at all.

'I wonder where the mine working is,' a voice said out of the darkness.

Frankie's hand slipped and she cut herself on glass. The sudden pain distracted her from a vision of a deep pit, the child lying at the bottom of it with beams and joists and all the rubble of the old house on top of her. Blood poured out of the gash.

'You need a stitch in that,' one of the policemen said. 'Come on love, I'll run you up to the hospital and bring you back. It's a nasty cut.'

It was something to do; to fill the hours; almost welcome and so was the pain, a distraction from a growing knowledge that no person trapped in a building like that had a chance of survival. They drove past Shallow Dene. She thought for one moment that she saw a man's shadow and then told herself off for being fanciful. There was no one there.

Behind them, at Tranter's, the men tried to work out where the cellar had opened. Sandy had told them how the child slipped inside, to look at the two small animals. Guilt overwhelmed her. What a purblind stupid fool she'd been, and at her age, too.

The men were working in silence, afraid of moving a beam or a door, and finding the child crushed beneath it. No one expected to see her alive. Sam avoided all of them, working at the edge of the garden on one of the corners, his mind blank, his expression bleak. It was best to be occupied, to work on, no matter what would happen, rather than to stand useless, wondering, feeling hopelessness usurp all other emotions.

He had a sudden vision of Shanie flying out of the house, cannoning into him, racing to get to Spencer's car so that she

113

shouldn't be late to school; laughing as she played with the pup, kneeling, totally absorbed, bottle-feeding the little pigs. Waiting beside him, excitement in her eyes, her hand gripping his, as the calves were born, always treating each as a recurring miracle, while the cow dipped her head to look at this creature she had so mysteriously brought into the world.

The child would have made a perfect farmer.

Thought gave way to sudden swift and savage action. He had to get through the rubble; had to comfort her or hold her hand. She was only a baby still; not yet thirteen; such a short time to live.

There was a noise on the air, a scream of terror and a bellow of rage.

The night had gone swiftly mad.

Sandy paused, and stared towards Sam, who had dropped the brick he was holding and was racing into the lane. Dear God, the bull had got loose, and there would be all hell to pay. Hannibal was never sweet tempered at the best of times, and tonight, frightened by all the noise around him, he would be a fiend from hell.

The policemen straightened themselves and pounded after Sam. Their heavy footsteps died away.

But the screams continued, on and on and on.

Tam and Mac had heard of the trouble at Tranter's and had joined Ken. They watched, almost gleeful, just standing, and Mac wandered off down the lane towards the farm. He returned and found Ken and Tam standing under a tree, smoking. There seemed little to do and everything was under control, but disaster fascinated them. They would have watched hangings if there had still been public spectacles when men died. As it was, there were always road accidents and burning buildings, and there was always the chance of loot.

But not tonight, with nothing to steal from Tranter's.

'There's nobody at the farm,' Tam whispered. 'And the mare's in the stable. I can hear her tramping in the straw.'

Ken looked around him. Nobody would leave for hours. Frankie had been driven away to the hospital. Sam and Sandy and Cuckoo were working as if possessed. The men from the building site were directing operations, moving carefully, aware of the danger of another fall, of unseen pits beneath them, of subsidence of the whole building, taking them with it, of disaster compounded upon disaster. They had seen too much and worked in too many places to be careless here.

If Tam led the mare to the edge of the far fields, Ken could have the horse box there within the hour. No one would even notice till morning and by then he would be off down the motorway. He could be in Exeter in six hours. No trace would be left. They would take good care of that. And no trouble this time; nothing to associate the theft with the vandalism. They had to be in the clear.

No one saw them leave. Few of the men had even noticed them, standing inconspicuously in the shadows. Everyone was far too preoccupied. Ken was part of the scenery and hoped everyone would believe he had been helping move bricks all night. No one had set eyes on Tam or Mac. Tich was still in hospital as he had broken his pelvis as well as fracturing his skull. His fingerprints had been identified as being among those on the farm that Saturday and when he recovered there would be charges to answer. Tich would be no use to them again.

Ken looked about him. Lights were on in the farmhouse kitchen but the room was empty. Pip barked, her voice muted by the brick walls. No one would take any notice of a dog, that night. There was plenty to make it bark.

He looked down the lane. Darkness until they reached Tranter's. Silence and no sound of footsteps. He knew everyone on the farm and the place was as deserted as a graveyard at midnight. He walked into the yard and Pip increased her noise and was echoed by the puppy's shriller voice.

There was a movement inside the stable.

Ken had a swift vision of the mare, of her bright coat and wise head and the foal beside her, of the man who would pay good money for both and see mother and foal safely out of the country. It was easy enough from Plymouth. Jack Mason had an export business and no one would notice if one horse was substituted for another. A good 'un instead of a decrepit nag destined for the French petfood trade, too ropy even to find its way to the dinner tables of those who liked horseflesh instead of beef.

The padlock was solid and would take some smashing, but there was enough noise from Tranter's to mask the sounds, as bricks were flung on to the lorry that was to take them away and men called to one another. Jackson and Johnson, still in Spencer's estate wagon, began to echo the dogs' barking. Everyone would think they were barking at the crashes in the night.

Ken had a heavy spanner with him.

He smashed it down on the padlock.

The lock broke, and he opened the door. A warm smell of animal came from inside, and Tam and Mac crowded up against him to take care that this time the mare did not stampede, and evade them.

The bull had been uneasy all evening. He hated noise, and he was aware of a cow ready for him in a stall nearby. He had not been given his last feed of the day. Sam had forgotten him in his anxiety. The stable door had been shut fast for far too long.

Hannibal was hidden in the shadows.

They were only aware of a dark bulk, its back towards them.

The final slam against his own door had maddened him beyond control.

He charged, his horns catching Ken full in the chest, throwing the man against Tam who crashed to the ground. Mac ran.

Hannibal paused to toss first one man and then the other across the yard. Anger mastered him, and he vented all his hatred on both, so that Ken hit his head heavily against the stone horse trough that Frankie kept filled with flowers; and Tam was flung like a lump of hay against the concrete wall of the pig sty where Trouble was charging about in fury.

The ganders, shut in the barn, cackled loudly.

The dogs barked, on and on and on.

Hannibal saw Mac's running figure and charged towards him. Mac was penned between the sties, having run the wrong way in panic. He had never liked animals, and to find himself faced by an enraged bull was the realization of a nightmare. His foot slipped, and he skidded head first into the midden.

Hannibal put his horns between the man's legs and flung him into the air, and caught him again. Mac, blinded by muck, his nose clogged, choking and sick with pig manure all over him, twisted away, and this time the bull caught him fairly in the chest and pinned him against the wall.

Mac was still screaming when the men reached the yard.

Sam and Cuckoo raced for the pitchforks and drove the bull away. The policemen called for ambulances. Hannibal, exhausted by his own ferocity, was led meekly back to his stall, but the broken lock made it impossible to shut him in and Sam led him to the old bull pen and fastened the yoke, leaving the half door open.

'They were after my mare,' he said flatly, as one of the policemen washed the muck off Mac's face. He was silent now, unable to breathe for the pain in his crushed and broken ribs. The bull had punished him severely. Ken and Tam were both unconscious, having struck their heads. The yard looked like a battlefield and the endless barking of the dogs added to the horror.

'Where is the mare?' one of the policemen asked.

'I sent her away,' Sam said. 'I guessed that was what they wanted. I reckon they took it out on the farm that day because she got away.'

'What was the bull doing in the stable?' asked the older man.

Sam shrugged.

'We were going to rebuild his pen. Seemed like the best place,' he said.

An ambulance came along the lane, a second vehicle following it. Sam walked away. He didn't even care.

His thoughts had gone back to Tranter's where Shanie lay under the rubble. He wouldn't have cared if the mare had been there and been stolen.

He would never care about anything any more.

He walked back down the lane, dimly aware of the departing ambulance, of Cuckoo beside him, of the barking of the agitated dogs.He ought to go and quiet them but there was no one there to hear.

He stood for a moment with Sandy, drinking the coffee that she had been home to make. The liquid warmed him but it tasted of nothing.

He put down the cup and walked over to the corner on which he had been working, and rolled up his shirt sleeves, having shed his coat in spite of the now persistent rain.

He had defeated his enemies but was not even aware of the fact.

CHAPTER SEVENTEEN

THERE was a path cleared to the cellar window. Bricks had fallen through, piling on the floor below, choking the entrance. It was like the sea coming over the sand, Sandy thought drearily, a remorseless tide blocking the way to the child. She couldn't possibly be alive. She couldn't have had a chance. Sandy thought of Shanie sitting in the cellar, the kitten and the cub beside her, and the sudden crash and rumble, the fall of the rafters and joists and beams, the twisting spill of bricks, the overhanging dust. The doom of Tranter's. She should have moved the little animals. It was ridiculous to keep them there, but the child had so adored her secret and she had seen no harm in it.

Seven for a secret never to be told.

. She remembered the magpies clearly; the wood and the birds' parliament and Shanie quoting the old magpie rhyme. The child's face was suddenly vivid in front of her. Sandy slipped into the darkness beyond the lights and leaned against a tree trunk.

The deep voice behind her made Sandy jump. She had not heard the policeman come.

'The little girl's alive,' he said.

Sandy looked at him blankly. She was so tired that the words didn't make sense.

'The child's alive,' he repeated.

Sandy followed him back to the pile of rubble, picking her way among broken tiles from the roof. Frankie had just arrived back from the hospital. Sandy made her way across the littered grass, feeling a lightening of the atmosphere that was damped when Cuckoo said it was impossible to reach her yet. There were great beams in the way and they didn't know how to pull them out as they held the floor up above her.

'Shanie,' Sandy called.

'I'm all right,' the small voice answered, exhausted and faint, but with no sign of panic. 'Only I'm trapped, right under the stairs. I put Tuska and Tomas in a basket. I'm so hungry,' she added forlornly.

'Can you see the lights, lovey?' Cuckoo called.

'Yes. You won't go away?'

'Nobody's going away,' one of the policemen said. The men were grinning at one another. It was only a matter of time and care; the child was safe and sounded in fairly good shape.

The little dark foreman returned them to reality.

'I don't think we dare go in to her from this side,' he said. 'If we move the two big joists to clear the way the floor will come down and everything above it. We'll have to try and clear the way to the cellar door and tackle it from there.'

'Can't I try to wriggle through to her?' Sandy asked. 'I'm the smallest of all of you.'

'Too dangerous,' the foreman said. 'You stay here and talk to her, while we work from the other side. Tell her we're doing our best. Anyone got a torch?'

One of the policemen came forward, holding a big hand-lamp. The foreman bent and shone it into the gap, taking care not to dislodge anything in front of him.

'Listen, love,' he called. 'Can you see what's in front of you?'

'Great lumps of wood,' Shanie said. 'Lying across each other. There isn't a gap anywhere.'

'Are you hurt?' Sandy asked.

'A brick banged my head and my hands hurt,' Shanie said. 'Not badly. I can move all of me, but my legs are so cramped. My head aches and it's dusty. I've sneezed till my nose bled. And it's dark.'

'We won't be long, love,' the foreman said.

He stood up, and looked at the men clustered around him.

'It's dodgy,' he said, in a low voice. 'Damned dodgy.'

'Can't you reach her quickly?' Sandy asked. 'She's cold and hungry ... there's danger of exposure. It's chilly to-night.'

'Can't risk it,' the man said flatly. He trudged off, and Sandy was left alone, standing useless beside the gap in the ground as unable to reach Shanie as if she had been on the moon.

'Sandy?'

Sandy crouched on the ground, trying to see into the darkness.

'I'm here, lovey.'

'Is Dad there?'

'He's helping move some of the brickwork above you. There's a long way to go yet.'

'Don't go away,' the small voice said, grabbing at the chance to talk, at a voice to ease the loneliness and the sheer terror that had been riding her ever since the house fell down. It had been an accident of fate, one of the things that happened to houses like Tranter's. She had just tied the basket to keep the cub and the kitten safe when the first rumble came, and had run into the cavity under the stairs, aware of impending danger. It had been terrifying crouching there, the basket with the crying animals under her school blazer, which she had put across it to save the tiny creatures from the choking dust.

She had known, all along, that they would find her, that it was only a matter of time. She had screamed when the bricks first began to fall, when the roof had slithered and tiles had rained outside the window. If she could have escaped then she would have been safe but the whole house was moving, and it was much too dangerous. The dark had been the worst part of it; the dark and the dust and the strange noises; were the ghosts of Tranter's lying around her, moving, angry at the changes that had come to their home? Once she thought she heard a piper, thin and far away, coming closer. She was so hungry and so thirsty and her head throbbed. She drifted once into unconsciousness. It had been a hearty crack on the skull. She woke to hear people moving overhead, to hear the slip and scurry of dust shifting and falling around her, rising in little eddies, choking her again. Her mouth and throat were filled with grit, her eyes ached, where she had to rub them clean with a handkerchief that was as dusty as she. She dared not open the basket.

'Sandy, have you gone away?' Shanie asked.

'I'm here, lovey,' Sandy said. She was half sitting, half lying, across the bricks, feeling them dig into her, bruising her, while the rain added penance by beginning again, at first only a thin drizzling but soon replaced by an uncomfortable steady downpour. It was impossible to think of anything to say.

'Sing, Sandy,' Shanie said.

Sing? Sing, here in the rain and the dark bedevilled by fear? Sing while the men worked and the bull bellowed and the cow answered and Frankie sat, dizzy, in the police car, nursing a bandaged hand which was far more severely cut than anyone had realized? Sing what?

She could only think of nursery rhymes. Every song she had ever known had gone from her head.

Somewhere beyond the trees light was dawning. Unbidden, the words came to her lips, of Shanie's favourite song.

> Morning has broken,
> Like the first morning . . .

She sang it to the end and sang it again. The men were coming nearer, and one of the policemen, realizing what she was doing, picked up the words, and when she had ended, he began his own song.

> Old Man River,
> He runs for ever,
> Just keeps on rolling . . .

The other men joined in, singing softly, singing to banish fear and to comfort a small girl, crouched alone in a dusty cellar, chilled and hungry and unable to move in the dark. Cuckoo had worked until he was forced to rest. Time drifted away and he was a young man again, courting. He had a grand voice then, when he was in his pomp. He had often sung to his bride. Pretty as a kitten she'd been and he suddenly remembered her singing to the baby. He had sung too; the pair of them side by side, proud with new parenthood. Not a penny to spare in those days, poorer than ever anyone was now they'd been, but it had never mattered. There was always home-made bread on the table and home-made jam and butter from Shallow Dene. What had that song been again that the baby had always loved, looking up at them from vivid blue eyes, watching them both? Nothing ever like your first bairn. Roger was in Australia now. And Cuckoo had never seen his grandchildren. His second child had died at birth and there were no more.

Cuckoo heaved himself out of the car and walked over to join Sandy. The singing had faltered. They had run out of tunes and out of ideas. Cuckoo's voice was gritty, but as he began to sing the others took up the tune, and Shanie, listening, curled close against the basket, slipped into an exhausted sleep, lulled by the words.

Sleep, my little one,
Sleep my pretty one,
Sleep my little one,
Sleep.

'She'll be all right. She's a tough little girl,' Spencer said to Sam, as they shifted bricks, working in a daze of weariness. It had been a very long night.

Sandy shifted her position and looked about her. Day was more than a rumour now. The clouds were breaking and colour was returning to the world. Star came to join her. The cat had seen the house fall and had fled, terrified, to hide in the barn under the hay. Later, she ran purposefully down the lane, and then crouched behind the hedge, horrified to discover that there were men and cars and floodlights all around the place, and that she could not reach her kitten and her cub.

She slipped through the hedge into the field and approached cautiously. The cat was relieved to find Sandy beside the gap, humming softly, having exhausted her memory and her voice. Star rubbed against Sandy's leg and ran towards the cellar opening. Everything had changed. She came back to Sandy to rub frantically against her, asking for comfort.

'Oh, Star,' Sandy said forlornly. 'Do you realize this is all your fault?'

Sam, walking wearily across the uneven ground, overheard her.

'Shanie?' he called softly, a question in his voice.

'I think she must have fallen asleep,' Sandy said. 'She sounded surprisingly perky. She's an astounding child, Sam. She's made no fuss at all.'

'Aye,' Sam said. 'I've been finding out.'

'Dad?' Shanie, waking, heard her father's voice. It was immensely reassuring to know that he and Sandy were there.

'I'm here, lass,' Sam said. He knelt and spoke into the dark. 'We'll have you out of there in no time at all.'

He turned his head as the foreman tapped him on the shoulder.

'We can't get in that way,' he said. 'We'll have to do what we can from here. But we've got problems.'

The floodlights dimmed and died. The tractor engine grumbled to a stop. Day had come, lightening the fields. Sam realized with a guilty start that it was past milking time and the cattle were lowing. He would have to go. Nobody would do it for him. No matter what happened, come day, go day, world end too, the cows had to be milked.

The foreman and three of the men were already discussing what they should do. Sam turned to walk down the lane, his eyes aching with lack of sleep. He turned his head. On a tree beyond Tranter's a blackbird sang. Underneath was desolation. Suppose after all that they made a mistake. It didn't bear thinking about. He went home and released Pip. The pup had puddled on the carpet. No time to clean up. He closed the door downstairs, crossed the yard and Pip trotted through the gate to collect the cows and bring them to her master.

CHAPTER EIGHTEEN

DAY did not improve the scene. Sandy looked around her. Beyond the overgrown garden the trees in the park stood sharp against the sky, stark against heavy cloud. There was not yet enough light to colour the leaves. The world was a drab cold grey, the clouds an over-arching pall, promising even more rain. She was cold and she hugged herself. The men had stopped to drink coffee that Cuckoo had made and Spencer had brought down in his car. Jackson and Johnson sat with astounded faces, watching the unusual scene. Sandy looked into the cellar. The heavy beams hid Shanie completely, lying tumbled against one another, leaning drunkenly, supporting a floor that looked increasingly perilous. Bricks lay above the ground. The foreman did not want anyone walking over that area.

Bricks were piled around them, flung well away from the site of the house. Sandy thought that there was nothing more desolate than a ruined house, and somehow Tranter's looked far more empty than it ever had standing. The wind rustled in the wet grass.

Sandy drank coffee and ate a sandwich that tasted of grit and dust. Her hands were bleeding, the nails broken, the skin filthy. Her arms were gooseflesh. Her hair was full of dust when she ran her fingers through it. But she wasn't going home. Not while the child needed her. She lowered herself through the cellar window, and crouched, holding a torch, trying to see into the cracks.

'Who's there?' Shanie asked.

'Sandy, lovey. All right?'

'I wish I could stretch,' Shanie said. 'My legs've got cramp and there's nowhere to move them. It's an awfully small place,' she added, a fretful note in her voice.

'Soon be out,' a voice said behind Sandy. The foreman had lowered himself into the cellar and was looking at the joists.

'We'll have to prop that floor before we try and reach you, but we ought to be able to get a drink of hot soup to you before then. Won't be long,' he added, and hoisted himself out again.

There were cries from the two small animals.

'Tuska and Tomas are hungry,' Shanie said. 'They keep crying. I wish I could see if they're all right.'

'Better not open the basket, lovey,' Sandy said. 'They may jump out and with all this noise about we'd lose them. They'll be terrified. Is the lid safe?'

'I tied my belt round it,' Shanie said. 'It won't open. I'll give it to you as soon as I can. It's such a long time.' There was a quiver in her voice. Sandy sat herself down and tried to think of something to talk about.

'Are the stairs stone or wood?' the foreman asked.

'Stone,' Shanie said, a disembodied voice coming out of the darkness.

'Good.'

'Why?' Shanie asked.

The foreman had gone away.

'Less likely to collapse,' Sandy said. If those stairs had been wooden the child would be dead. Miracles did happen. They would be able to get Shanie out.

'Please talk,' the small remote voice said.

There was nothing left to say, and Sandy was tired. She began to recite.

'I will lift up mine eyes unto the hills,'

'From whence cometh my help.' Shanie joined in, glad of

an occupation, however small. She had learned the psalm at school.

Sandy completed the psalm and started on another. The police cars drove away. A lorry loaded with pit props arrived and parked and the driver got down to talk to the foreman, who came back to the cellar a few minutes later.

'We'll talk to her while we work,' he said. 'Go on home and get some rest, Miss. There's nothing you can do now. You get some sleep. It's just a matter of time.'

'How long?' Sandy asked. Time had become meaningless. The night had been unending, like nights spent when ill, the slow clock refusing to show the passing hours, only the minutes, so that each thought occupied an eternity.

The foreman shrugged expressively, flinging wide his hands, but his voice when he spoke was cheerful.

'Not long now. We'll have the lass out in no time at all, Miss. Don't you worry.'

'See you later, lovey,' Sandy called. 'I must go and feed the cats.'

'See you,' Shanie's voice said, but the tone was forlorn.

'There's going to be four of us down here working to get you out,' the foreman said. 'We're a right noisy lot, full of good ideas and jokes. We'll be there in no time at all. Don't worry if you hear crashes. It's only the props falling through the gap here. We want to prop that roof and make sure it doesn't fall on your head. O.K.?'

'O.K.,' Shanie said.

Sandy clambered out and walked down the garden path, that had been cleared to make a way to the gate. The lane was muddy after the rain. Hannibal had stopped bellowing. The fields were empty. Sam must be finishing milking and hadn't yet put the cows out. She called in at Shallow Dene. Sam was about to take the cows down the lane. She patted Bossgirl on her black and white nose and stroked Lisalou. Both of them were Shanie's favourites, trotting up to the child to be petted and fussed, asking for titbits. They both loved pony nuts and Shanie always kept some in her pocket.

Sandy stroked Bossgirl's nose as if her life depended on it. Her brain seemed to have ceased functioning. It was time to go home and feed her own cats. Time to turn away, to walk down the lane, to think of other things, but her thoughts remained with Shanie.

'If the vandals hadn't killed the animals,' Sandy said,

unable to hold her tongue, unable to stop, wishing the clock back. If the farm had been left in peace none of it would have happened. Shanie would be safe.

'What do you think I've been thinking all night?' Sam asked. He looked at Sandy, defeated. His face was grey with exhaustion, the unshaven stubble also rough and grey against his reddened skin. 'But the bull settled the score. Those three won't be back. I'll get Cuckoo to strengthen the place for her animals. She's been trying to do it herself. If I'd noticed before I'd have wondered what was up.'

He led the way to the back of the barn, where a pen had been made a long time ago for a bitch Sam had once owned. There was a large kennel, and a double enclosure with an outer door and an inner door to ensure that the puppies could never escape. It was mended in an amateur fashion, nails and wood all awry.

'If you'll let her keep that kitten, I'll pay you his market price,' Sam said, knowing Siamese didn't grow under bushes though by the sound of it this one had almost been born under one.

'She can have a thousand kittens for free,' Sandy said.

There was a faint sheen behind the cloud as the sun tried to break through. A cat sauntered lazily across the yard. Hannibal lowed. It was near to his feeding time. Sam had put him with the cow to quieten him. They were in a paddock behind the barn. The bull's anxious face peered over the gate. He only knew the certainty of his routine and today nothing was happening at the right time. The bitch was hungry too, but knew she had to be patient.

Sandy walked wearily home.

There was too much to do. Earth boxes to empty and scald and refill; food to prepare; and she must eat too. She was so tired that each job took an age, mocking her with the necessity to do it properly, to ensure no cats escaped, to check on the health of her charges. Ordinarily this was a job she performed with love but today the cats maddened her, clamouring for extra attention because she had been away all night and they had been locked in. No need for that any more. Cuckoo came to help, reporting briefly that they were propping up the floor and Shanie was quite cheerful.

'She's a game little maid,' he said.

The clock was still a creeping snail. The hands barely moved. She was living through a century, dragged by weariness, barely caring about herself. Cuckoo made coffee for both of them, and filled a plate with breakfast cereal and milk and put it in front of Sandy. She fed without noticing what she ate.

'Suppose they are wrong?' she said. 'About the props. That's a stone floor and the beams are rotten. We should never have gone in in the first place. I should have stopped her. I never thought . . .'

'That's been many a good man's epitaph,' Cuckoo said.

It wasn't any consolation at all.

CHAPTER NINETEEN

FRANKIE had been persuaded to go home and rest. The gash in her hand throbbed abominably. It had been far worse than she had thought, a long jagged cut requiring four stitches. An injection had added to her woes. Her arm ached and she felt sick through lack of food.

But rest was impossible.

The hospital had provided her with a sling to keep her arm still. It was her left hand and she was able to use her right to fill the kettle, turning on the tap first, splashing water over herself, and finding it difficult to plug in the wretched thing in. She brewed herself a cup of instant coffee, strong and black, and spooned in sugar, and drank, relishing the warmth. She was so cold.

She had been told of the bull's escape and the resultant shambles and felt nothing; no pity; no triumph. Only an infinite weariness, and a sense of futility. Men were so greedy and so stupid. She did not think these would return. The horses could come home. Or would the mare's presence attract other thieves, equally unscrupulous?

She ought to eat but cutting bread one-handed was impossible, and she couldn't grip the loaf, as the gash was right across the palm. She must have caught it on a piece of glass from a broken window. She hadn't been thinking; she should have been more careful. She wished that time would speed by; that the men would bring Shanie home. Suppose the child were hurt, after all. Sandy had said that she seemed unharmed but they didn't know.

She couldn't stay there. She had to know what was going on. She walked back down the endless lane.

There seemed to be more rubble than ever. The child couldn't be alive. Men were working, crawling around the cellar entrance, their actions totally without meaning. Frankie walked over to the nearest man. He was a stranger to her, come up that morning as part of a relief team to let those who had been working all night go home and bath and eat and rest. Some had not rested. They had returned and were helping again.

'Nothing to see here, Miss,' the man said abruptly. The police had cleared off two lots of sightseers who had been hampering the work. People would come and stare at anything. His voice was impatient.

'I'm the child's aunt,' Frankie said, in a small defeated voice. She wanted to go over to the gap and speak to Shanie, to hear her voice, to know for certain that the child was all right.

'I'm sorry, Miss,' the man said, suddenly compassionate. He looked at Frankie for the first time. Colour had drained from her face and her eyes were shadowed, the lids bruised with tiredness. The throbbing hand had etched lines of pain around her mouth. Her clothes were dusty from the night's work. She felt sick. She should have gone to bed. She had lost too much blood. The world was beginning to whirl.

The man put his arm around her, dirtying the clean white sling.

'The little girl's all right,' he said. 'We're nearly ready to bring her out. She's a great kid. The men have been teasing her and making her laugh. And there's a police dog in with her now. One of the handlers managed to send it through to keep her company. And to keep her warm. The dog knows its job. It's a good 'un.'

Sam had joined them. He and Cuckoo had finished the milking in record time and left the cleaning up. It could wait. Everything could wait. They had carried food to the animals, and put the pup in the stable where puddles did not matter. No one would disturb the farm now. At least that fear had gone

He glanced at his sister.

She wasn't fit for anything. She had forgotten to comb her

hair and there were streaks of dirt across her face and her clothes were filthy. Frankie was always fastidious. Her untidiness set a seal on the horror. The men were shoring up a giant beam. If the damned thing slipped . . .

Sam wanted to crawl beneath it and take all its weight on himself, wanted to rescue his own child. He resented the men who were near her.

'If you can make enough space for me to get through I could fetch her out,' Sam said.

'Boss sent a fellow down who used to put pit props in place in one of the local mines,' the ginger-head said. 'He's working there now, shoring it up. Be about half an hour, he said, before he can shift the beams that are blocking her.'

It was an endless half hour. Sam found a door that had come from the rubble, and propped it on several piles of bricks so that Frankie could sit and stay close. The work filled a few minutes. One of the police cars came back and the driver walked over to find out how the men were progressing, and to put in a report. He came over to stand beside Sam and watch. There was nothing to say.

The wind howled in the trees. Clouds tore across the sky, an endless dizzy procession in constant chase. Far away, a diesel train hooted, as it sped through a station without stopping. A plane roared overhead, temporarily drowning the noise of the wind. A man laughed, down in the cellar, and then his voice rose sharply as he called out.

'Steady. You'll have the whole lot down if you do that.'

Frankie clenched her teeth. Sam was sure she should not be there, but was grateful for her presence. You needed family as you got older. Someone who had shared a part of life with you; someone to call you by your given name and not stand on ceremony; someone who had laughed with you and quarrelled with you, and who knew more than most about the man behind the façade.

Sandy joined them, saying nothing either. There wasn't anything to say. There was an air of purpose now about the proceedings, as men worked swiftly, passing down the props to the man below. He kept up a constant light banter that was immensely cheering.

'Soon have you out; just put this one under there, and Bob's your uncle, that's another inch for me to crawl through. Lucky I'm only a little one. They say the best goods come in small packages but my mum thought I'd never be good for anything. Maybe make a jockey, but horses scare me stiff. All kicking hooves and biting teeth and they don't like the smell of me. You like horses, lovey?'

'We've got horses,' Shanie said. 'Only we haven't,' she added forlornly, remembering. The foal would be enormous now and even if she came back they'd have missed half of the fun of her, when she was small and bucked in the evening madness and sped round the field, kicking up her hooves and whinnying to her mother.

'Ah well, that's the way the cookie crumbles,' the man said, his mind not at all on his words, but on the patient skill with which he was tenderly inserting the baulk of wood, careful not to cause the slightest slip of the beam that lay across the child. He didn't like the look of it. One inch to the left or the right . . . and there were strange noises all the time.

He was used to working underground, using a sixth sense as guide, listening for the change of sound that spelled the end of safety, for the sharp crack of breaking wood, for the soft slur of shifting earth, for the tell-tale gurgle of intruding water. He was as sensitive as any scientific instrument, and all his craftsmanship was in the delicate touch of his gnarled and dirty fingers. He tapped the prop home and breathed a sigh of relief. But he wasn't finished yet, not by a long chalk.

'Another nail on the road to freedom,' he said. 'Have you out as quick as a bee's sneeze.'

Shanie giggled.

His name, he'd said, was Matt, and he was funny to listen to even if she was lying there cramped and so hungry she felt faint. Her hand stroked the police dog. Simba licked her. His presence was reassurance and company and the knowledge that he had got through the gap to her had comforted her more than anything else that had happened since the house collapsed. Matt had explained a little about the old mine workings. Not too much. He didn't want to frighten her, or to reveal his fear that the whole of the ground beneath them might give way again and all of them tumble God knew how far below.

And if that happened there was no hope for any of them; rescuers or rescued.

'How's that dog of mine behaving?' Duncan Strang asked, as the foreman began to work on yet another pit prop. The waiting was the worst part of it. There was nothing more any of them could do but keep out of the way and help to cheer the child. Most of the policemen had left. The rescue was in competent hands.

'He's good,' Shanie said. 'I've got a dog; a puppy. She's a golden retriever. Her name's Peppy. She's naughty.'

'Nothing like a good Alsatian,' Duncan said. 'Best dog in the world, treated right. They've got more sense in their noses than any other dog in their whole bodies. And Simba's more sense than most. He's so clever he can tell me if a man's a crook or not, can't you Simba?'

'Am I a crook?' Matt asked, his eyes flashing out of the darkness of his dirty face.

'Is Matt a crook?' Duncan asked.

The dog barked, making Shanie jump.

'Not too much of that,' Matt said. 'Might make something slip. Did the dog say yes or no?'

'He growls for yes,' Duncan said.

Shanie, lying in the tiny recess, watched the lights. They shone in her eyes and hid the men behind them, but first one prop and then another was put in place. When she tried to move she found her legs so stiff that they failed to obey her, and it was only when the last prop was in position and the light flooded through and shone over her legs that she realized that a beam lay across both of them, preventing her from any movement at all.

'Soup,' a voice said, and she looked up to see the policeman leaning over the beam, balancing himself on one hand on the floor, careful not to put any weight on the beam. He handed her a cup. 'Sip slowly, it's hot,' he said.

There was a squeal from beside him.

'It's only the kitten,' Shanie said. 'They hate being shut in.' The two animals were moving about inside the basket, grumbling to themselves. They were very hungry.

Slowly, light began to show from outside as the blocking rubble was moved.

'Room for a little one?' a voice asked.

The young doctor who crawled in beside her was beautifully dressed. His dove grey trousers and pale blue shirt and silver buttoned blazer would never be the same again. He took the soup from the policeman.

'I'll do this,' he said. 'It's just what the doctor ordered, isn't it, poppet? Those legs of yours. Do they hurt?'

Shanie shook her head.

'They feel stiff and I've got a sort of cramp in my right leg,' she said. 'It's just that I can't move.'

She finished the soup. It was warming and she immediately felt less tired. She had drifted in and out of sleep all night long. Her head ached and the doctor's exploring fingers found a long cut under the hair. He knelt to look at the beam and let out a deep sigh.

'She's jammed, is all,' he said to the foreman. The men had been working grimly, dreading what they might find when they reached the beam. Now all they had to do was to be very careful. The atmosphere lightened.

One of the men switched on a small transistor radio that he had put down by the cellar opening. Music flooded the cellar. The soft insistent rhythm was soothing, and Shanie, relieved from fear, and warmed by the soup, fell asleep, her head against the doctor's arm. He shifted so that he was sitting beside her, and eased her gently against his shoulder, holding her close, pondering on the oddities of his work that brought him few occasions as satisfying as this, when he was totally committed and absolutely necessary, and was bringing comfort. Life must have been much more satisfying before the bureaucrats got busy, he thought.

'Is she O.K.?' one of the men asked anxiously, startled to find the child could sleep so deeply with all the noise around her.

'She's dead beat,' the doctor said. 'Her legs are going to hurt like hell when you do get her out, but it will only be because they're cramped, with being in the same position for so long. There's no pressure on her. She was very lucky.'

Sam, who had been squatting at the end of the cellar, out of the way of the experts, watching, felt his spirits lift. He had not come in again until the doctor had made his examination, afraid of what he might hear. He wanted his daughter safely out of the cellar, wanted to put his arms around her, to hold her close, to bury his face in her hair, to tell her how much he needed her. Even as he thought this he knew he would never do it. He wasn't a man for pretty speeches. He was barely a man for words. It was hard to talk to anyone unless he could talk about the things he knew well; about seedtime and harvest; about cattle breeding and pig breeding; about the thousand and one fascinations he encountered daily on the farm and pondered about as he worked, sometimes talking them over with Cuckoo, but often keeping them to himself, in case he were laughed at. Strange things happened in the animal world and those who didn't know animals often wouldn't believe them.

He knew about animals by instinct; could handle any of them, could sense if they were unwell, though Shanie was better than he at that. She was his child; with his instincts and his interests. He wished he were small enough to climb through the gap and reach her. The doctor was a tiny man. Perhaps that was why the police had chosen him. Their own doctor was as big as Sam and could never have crawled into the gap.

'She's free,' one of the men said. 'Can you make sure those legs aren't broken?'

'They're fine,' the doctor said. He shook Shanie gently.

'Wake up, poppet. We're going to get you out of here.'

Shanie had forgotten how to move. She watched as the basket was lifted and handed to Sandy who was waiting for it, her face anxious. Shanie clung to the doctor and managed to shift her legs. They were so cramped and stiff that the movement made her feel sicker than ever.

'We've a stretcher here,' a voice said. 'There's an ambulance waiting outside.'

'I don't want to go to hospital,' Shanie wailed. She had managed to stay calm for the whole of the rescue operation, but the thought of leaving the animals, of not knowing how they were after their terrible night, was more than she could bear. Tears crept down her cheeks.

'Just for a check up,' the doctor said. 'And I want those cuts and scratches dressed and an X-ray of your head. That was a nasty bump. You'll need a day or two in bed anyway; it's not everyone who gets buried alive under a building that's fallen down.'

'I want to see Tomas and Tuska. I want to know they're all right,' Shanie said.

'I'll take them home and feed them,' Sandy promised. 'Look, if the policeman will give me a lift we can go quickly to the farm and release them in the cage you made, and Spencer can come and look them over. I'll tell you before you're in the ambulance just how they are. Or the ambulance can stop at the gate. O.K.?'

It had to be. Shanie nodded, and Sandy went off with the policeman who had been watching the final stages of the rescue operation. He was not needed, and this would do the child good.

'Kids are funny creatures,' he observed as he started the engine of the police car. 'I've got three of my own. You can't make out what goes on in their heads.'

It only took a few minutes to drive to the farm. The policeman followed Sandy and watched as she went into the old kennel. She opened the empty compartment and shut herself inside, shooting the bolt. The kitten and the cub were moving inside the basket, pushing and struggling, and a paw came up through the crack where the lid met the side. A fox paw she decided.

She opened the box and the two small animals exploded from it. They were covered in grime and dust, but neither showed any sign of harm. The kitten spat at her and the cub hissed, and she went out swiftly lest they attacked. The door to the run was open and they crept round the cage, sniffing every corner, and then crept to the doorway. The policeman moved, intrigued, and they fled back to the safety of the darker compartment, and crouched in the shadows, bewildered by their new surroundings. Sandy put food and water ready. They would eat when they were alone.

The ambulance was already at the gate. Sam, sitting beside his daughter, filled the inside.

'They're fine,' Sandy said. 'Scared, but they're O.K. I promise. You'll see them as soon as you come home.'

The ambulance door closed. Sandy watched the vehicle drive down the lane and turn out on to the main road. She had better help Cuckoo and see how Frankie was. She walked into the farmhouse.

Timbo materialized from the barn, where he had hidden when the bull escaped. He carried his stump tail high. When all was done, Sandy thought, the one reminder they would have of the awful summer and autumn was poor Timbo's amputated stump. It had healed but the fur had not grown and Spencer thought that it might stay naked for ever. It annoyed Timbo who licked at it savagely as if he could make it grow again.

Cuckoo had chased Frankie off to bed, using his tongue as a flail to goad her. He was busy at the range, making soup from a packet.

'Thought it would do her good. You can take it up,' Cuckoo said.

He yawned hugely.

'Never been so tired in my life. It's worse than being up with a calving cow. That's a funny carry on of Star's. Never seen a kitten and a cub play together before. Been watching them.'

He yawned again and poured the soup from the pan into a brown earthenware mug. Sandy took it upstairs, but Frankie was sound asleep and she hadn't the heart to wake her. She sat on the stool in the bathroom and drank the soup herself, not to disappoint Cuckoo, and then took the mug downstairs and washed it out.

There was a lot to do around the place. The memory of the night was on the table. Dirty cups and plates and saucers, and half a loaf. There were tongue marks on the butter. One of the cats. She would have to tidy up, but not for the moment.

She sat in the big wicker chair and kicked off the shoes that were tormenting her. Cuckoo had gone outside, and after some thought went home to rest, setting his alarm clock so that he would wake in good time to help clear up before the evening milking.

When Sam was brought home by a police car, having left Shanie asleep in bed at the hospital, he walked into a silent house. Sandy was sound asleep in the kitchen chair, all thoughts of clearing up forgotten.

Sam collected the cups and went out into the scullery to wash them up. He no longer felt tired. He had dozed in the car all the way home, and several of his problems had vanished with the night.

The bull had settled the vandals, once and for all. They would never return. Fear would see to that and their fingerprints had been identified. Tam and Mac had both been at the farm that Saturday afternoon. And Ken's presence was condemnation enough. And Sam was in no way liable. The bull had been in a padlocked stable and had not been loose. The men had released him and brought the trouble on themselves. Sam could prosecute for damage and trespass.

He walked back into the kitchen and hung the mugs on the dresser, careful to make no noise. Sandy was exhausted. She was old, Sam thought with sudden pity, looking at her as she lay back, defenceless, all character gone from her face.

She would rest easy now too. All of them would be safe.

135

Or as safe as was possible in these strange times. You could never be certain.

There was a piece of paper on the floor.

Sam picked it up and glanced at it and then knew, in a sudden sickening moment, that nothing was solved after all.

It was the tax demand.

£57,000.

He had forgotten all about it.

CHAPTER TWENTY

FRANKIE overslept.

When she came downstairs Sam had finished the milking, and had covered the table with files. He was frantically looking through all the back tax information; through the income on the milk each month; the sales receipts for cattle. It was quite impossible to lay the meal.

'I can't make it out,' he said irritably. 'Unless they made a mistake on the death duties; and surely to God those were high enough. They set us back for years. We'll never get them back; and even if I sell off all the stock, at today's prices, I can't make it. And there's enough owing at the bank. Look at the bill for the winter hay for the horses last year after the stacks went up. And I wonder who was responsible for that?' he added.

'Why don't you write and query it?' Frankie asked irritably, wondering why on earth it was that all the men she knew worried and worried at details and never did anything about them. They seemed to repeat the same conversation day after day without getting anywhere.

She clattered the dishes into the sink. Sam had made himself a bacon sandwich before going out to do the milking and left the plates for her. It wasn't easy, one-handed, but he continued to brood over his papers, while she dumped the plates and cup and saucer in the bowl and swilled the water over them.

She had never been so exhausted in her life. She shuddered, remembering the long night and day at Tranter's. It must have taken the nurses hours to clean Shanie up. The child was so covered in dust that she was unrecognizable when they brought her out.

Cuckoo came in with a load of papers under his arm.

'Hit the headlines all right,' he said, flinging them on to the table.

Sam turned them over, his mind still on his figures.

BULL FOILS THIEVES.

That was the local paper.

BURIED CHILD SAFE

was the headline in one of the biggest national papers, and the others varied between Shanie's escape, and the bull running wild in the farmyard.

Shepherd Dorton ducked his head as he walked into the room.

'Brought this for Shanie,' he said. He nodded at the papers. 'Made news all right, didn't we? You'll be having offers for that bull from the security firms.'

He chuckled, and put a parcel on the table.

'Can I look?' Frankie asked, touched by his solicitude.

Shepherd nodded.

Frankie opened the box. Inside was a china Shire horse, a gay painted cart attached to it. Shepherd made the carts for sale. He had added to the horse's harness a tiny red rosette with the words FIRST PRIZE written on it, beautifully made, in perfect detail.

'She'll love it,' Frankie said with conviction. 'Wouldn't you like to take it to her yourself?'

'Got to make up for lost time, or I would,' Shepherd said. He nodded awkwardly. 'Glad the child's all right. You were pretty lucky,' he added as he went outside again.

Lucky, Frankie thought and then realized just how lucky they had been. The child might have been smothered by dust; it was a miracle she hadn't. If she hadn't been in the recess under the stairs she would have been killed by falling timber; if the floor hadn't been stone, and at that particular place, built over rock, she'd have fallen a hundred feet or more. The rear portion of the cellar had collapsed into the old workings. They had been lucky.

She began to prepare the food for the pigs. Everything

took three times as long as usual and her hand hurt more than ever. She rang the hospital. Shanie was asleep. No injuries, except for the cut on her head and a number of bad bruises. The child could probably come home next day.

Which was going to be complicated, Frankie thought; though she could borrow Sam's estate car, she couldn't drive, not with so sore a hand. And they had all yesterday's work to catch up on, as well as today's. She would have to hire a taxi and that meant spending unnecessary money.

'The horses can come back,' Sam said, thinking to ease his sister's misery, but only succeeding in compounding it, as she could not imagine how she could manage one-handed with more stock to care for. She was convinced the hand would go septic. It ached so much and the glass had been filthy.

There was a long yowl from outside, and a sharp unusual bark. She had forgotten about the cub and the kitten and both were hungry. She didn't know what to give them. Did foxes eat cat food? She rang Sandy, but Sandy had gone shopping and there was no reply. She rang Spencer, but he was out, at a calving.

She opened a tin of dogfood and took it outside. It would probably upset them, but she had to do something about the noise which was increasing. They hadn't been fed for nearly forty-eight hours, as no one had thought to give them extra the night before, and the meal that Sandy had set them had only been a hasty token.

Light shone into the barn through a high window. The kitten was lean and sleek. Both animals had spent the night washing themselves clean. Frankie, who had not been interested in them to any great extent, was suddenly fascinated, as they came towards her, half tame and very hungry. The kitten rubbed against the wire and purred. The cub was sharp eared and sharp nosed, watching her with bright attentive eyes, waiting to see the plate put down on the floor. She opened the door a crack and slipped the two plates inside.

Hunger mastered fear and both animals began to eat, Within seconds the kitten's plate was empty. The cub, his meal almost finished, squatted over his plate and fouled the food.

'He's going to be a problem,' Frankie said irritably to Cuckoo.

'That's fox habit. They always do that and nothing will

cure them,' Cuckoo said. 'Leastways, all those I've known. Had one myself when I was a youngster. Kept it for two years but it went savage on us. Wouldn't be told and fought the dogs, so it had to go. Me Dad took it down to Dartmoor and let it loose there so it wouldn't come back. Though I bet the other foxes chased it off. Always regretted losing that fox.'

The cub and the kitten began to play, shadow boxing round the cage. Excitement grew until the kitten, losing his temper, bit the cub's ear. The cub bit back, and an immediate fight ensued. Cuckoo clapped his hands and the two animals separated, running to opposite corners of the cage, the kitten spitting and the cub hissing.

'Going to be problems if they're kept together,' Cuckoo said.

Problems. You never got away from them. Solve one and another took its place. Shanie had set her heart on keeping the cub. Even Frankie was tempted, but it wouldn't do. Not with chickens about. And it might go for the dogs; and it might prove vicious.

Spencer called in later that morning with a book for Shanie, and a basket for the kitten to sleep in. He promised to collect the child from hospital himself, if Sam weren't free; it was his half-day and his practice was covered by a friend at the other end of the town.

He stood looking at the cub.

'It's not going to be possible to keep him,' Frankie said.

'And how do you tell that to the child?' Spencer asked, agreeing with Frankie but aware of the difficulties that lay ahead.

Shanie came home.

The problem of the fox cub remained unsolved, but even Shanie, seeing how he always fouled the remains of his food, felt that he would prove an awkward pet. The plates had to be rinsed under the tap in the yard and the smell was unpleasant. The rank foxy odour hung round the kennel; and the dogs hated him.

The mares came home, both now with foals. The hunter and Kelpie came too and there was a joyful reunion. The youngest, a little filly, was only a few days old. Shanie watched her run and jump, and the child made friends all over again with Tomboy, who had grown to a leggy six months old, racing with her shadow. Her mother still protected her, pushing her away from the second mare, Leda, totally jealous, never allowing her to play with the new foal.

Within days the mare was exhausted, protecting the filly from imaginary dangers, chivvying her from one end of the field to the other when she tried to socialize with Shanie.

'They've spoilt her,' Shanie said regretfully, as Vayla refused to come, even for pony nuts.

'She'll have been on her own, that's all,' said Frankie. She was only half listening to the child, her mind on the telephone. Their accountant was due to ring. Sam had discovered from his secretary that he was flying home the day before and he had booked an urgent call.

The ringing bell startled her, although she was expecting it. She left Shanie watching the kitten play with the cub and went into the kitchen where Sam was already talking.

He put down the receiver and stared at his sister.

And started to laugh.

'Are you all right?' Frankie asked acidly.

Sam picked up the demand note, which was written in ink. He crossed out the figure of £57,000 pounds and rewrote the sum.

£570.00.

Frankie was suddenly furious. All their agony and worry because someone had been careless and had fed in the wrong information into the computer, hadn't bothered to check. And yet, the answer was so obvious. Sam was still laughing. Relief had made him light-headed.

'Why didn't we think of that?' Frankie asked.

Sam shrugged.

'You don't, do you? Tax demands; electricity bill; gas bill; you take them for gospel. I reckon we ought to celebrate saving all that money.'

There was a loud wail from the yard.

Sam and Frankie ran outside, to find Shanie chasing after the fox cub. He slipped through the fence and was away over the fields. The kitten sat and washed himself, and stalked serenely across the yard and into the kitchen, where he settled himself by the warmth of the Aga and stared into space, his blue eyes almost crossing.

'I wanted to see what they'd do if I let them out,' Shanie said, disconsolate. She looked across the empty fields, and then at the soiled plate inside the kennel, and sighed deeply, all visions gone. She would never walk through the town with a fox on a lead; or play with him on summer nights, when he could romp with the dogs.

'It's for the best, love,' Frankie said, wishing the cub had stayed a little longer. But this solved everything, and the animal had every chance of surviving.

'It's for the best,' Cuckoo said too when he heard of the escape. 'I'll cheer you up, girl. Tell you a secret.'

'When?' Shanie asked.

'Tonight, when you're in bed,' Cuckoo said.

Shanie stared at him, astonished.

'How can you?' she asked. Cuckoo was going home at six that evening. He had been working overtime for weeks, in an effort to get everything topsides before winter.

'You'll see,' Cuckoo said.

That night, Peppy lay quiet beside the bed, and Tomas, investigating houses and finding them good, made himself a corner beside Shanie, snuggling up to her, purring loudly, so that she did not regret the cub's departure quite so much. She watched him lick himself clean and lay wondering how Cuckoo could tell her a secret at this time of night.

Very softly down the lane came the sound of bagpiping. The lilt of a lament; the call of a ballad; the skirl of a march and with it came the tramp of feet. Shanie ran to the window and looked out.

There was no one there.

She watched. A shadow materialized from under the trees, and terror caught her throat. There was a ghost out there; a Scotsman in full regalia, with a glittering brooch at the angle of his plaid and a shine on him like nothing in the world.

The pipes began again and the Scotsman marched into the yard.

Shanie stared, too terrified to scream. She wanted to run, but her legs refused to move. She wanted to shout, but her throat had closed. She longed for Sam and Frankie to come up the stairs and reassure her. There couldn't be anything there. She was dreaming.

A dog detached itself from the shadows. A collie. Cuckoo's rescued bitch. It barked and leaped at the figure, tail waving ecstatically. The bonnet was doffed and with a deep bow, the piper looked up.

'Cuckoo!'

Shanie raced downstairs, hastily buttoning her dressing gown. Cuckoo was in the kitchen, and Frankie had glasses of whisky ready for the men and sherry for Shanie and herself.

'Here's to our ghost,' she said.

'I thought it might scare off the crooks,' Cuckoo said. 'It was meant to add to all the creepy noises at Tranter's, but I don't reckon it did much good.'

'We all had secrets,' Shanie said. 'My cub and my kitten; and Cuckoo piping; and Dad, what was your secret?'

'The bull in the stable,' Sam said. 'I thought it would scare them off; I didn't expect it to do so much damage. But they won't be bothering us again.'

Shanie looked out into the fields where the horses were dark beneath the trees. The lane brooded, peaceful again. She could walk freely, but she knew there would always be a doubt; a stab of memory, fear lest strangers were hiding in the bushes, lest vandals returned again to the farm, lest her animals were harmed.

Tomas had come looking for her and jumped into her arms. She held him and he arched his back and lifted his chin and she remembered the black kittens. They would have been grown by now and running around.

'What's your secret, Frankie?' Shanie asked abruptly, seeing her aunt sitting, silent.

Frankie looked at her niece, and smiled.

'Never tell a secret,' she said. Her thoughts had been far away; twelve years away, when she had been free and when life might have been different.

Sandy came into the room, knocking sharply before she opened the door.

'I heard piping,' she said. 'Cuckoo, it *was* you.'

'You didn't really think there was a ghost?' Cuckoo asked her, and she shook her head.

'All the same, one night, I did wonder,' she added. 'I didn't even know you could play the bagpipes.'

'That was another secret,' Cuckoo said. 'We've all got secrets tonight. Miss Frankie isn't telling. Perhaps you'll share one with us?'

Sandy was looking at the kitten. She had not seen him cleaned up and in full light before. He gazed at her and stretched a slim leg and washed himself. Everyone was waiting for her to speak.

Sandy shook her head.

She had given the kitten to Shanie. She looked at him again and felt an ache in her throat. She had given away the best kitten that she had ever bred, that anyone had ever bred. He was gorgeous.

But that, too, was a secret, never to be told.

THE END

JOYCE STRANGER NOVELS AVAILABLE IN CORGI PAPERBACKS

THE PRICES SHOWN BELOW WERE CORRECT AT THE TIME OF GOING TO PRESS (FEBRUARY '83)